# TEQUILA BAY

## By Nigel Robinson

Based on three original
*Baywatch* scripts,
*Tequila Bay*, *Rookie of the Year*, and *Pier
Pressure*

B▣XTREE

First published in the UK 1993
by BOXTREE LIMITED, Broadwall House,
21 Broadwall, London SE1 9PL

10 9 8 7 6 5 4 3 2 1

Cover and insert photographs: Kim Carlsberg

Cover design by Nigel Davies at Titan Studio

1–85283–852–3

Phototypeset by Intype, London
Printed and bound in Great Britain by
Cox and Wyman Ltd.,
Reading, Berkshire

A catalogue record for this book is available from the
British Library.

# Prologue

*Man, is she ever beautiful*, thought Jimmy Slade, as he felt the sea breeze blow through his thick brown hair, and the first warm rays of the morning sun shine down on his tautly muscled body.

Out there in Tequila Bay the Pacific Ocean rushed relentlessly up onto the shore, creating some of the finest surfing waves in the whole of Southern California, and the entire world. The air was filled with the sound of the surf as it crashed and pounded mercilessly on the rocks, drowning out the squawks and cries of seabirds as they wheeled and gyred in the morning breeze. Slade breathed in the clean smell of ozone, that bracing smell which made such a difference to the smog-polluted atmosphere of the big city.

The Pacific was blue, bluer than Slade had ever seen it before, flecked with crests of snow-white foam, and sparkles of golden sunlight. Out beyond Tequila Bay he could see nothing on the horizon, just one unending stretch of all-encompassing water, the hugest, most beautiful, most awesome ocean in the entire world.

*Man, is she ever beautiful*, Slade repeated to himself, and added whimsically: *If you sailed out there far and long enough, the next big chunk of land you'll reach is gonna be Japan*!

He looked behind, at the battered old transit van which he had parked a little way up the shore; and then past the van to the concrete skyscrapers of Los Angeles, the wealthiest city in the wealthiest state of the United States of America.

In the early-morning sun the glass-fronted towers glinted and gleamed, and Slade had to admit that even they possessed an odd sort of beauty.

He turned back to the ocean, and grinned. *Heck! There's just no contest*!

The ocean was where Jimmy Slade belonged, the place he felt most at home. Riding on the crest of the waves gave him such a buzz, made him feel as much a part of the wide and wonderful Pacific Ocean, as the rainbow-coloured fish, or the soaring seabirds high above his head.

And he was wasting time!

Grabbing his customised surfboard which he'd leant up against the side of his van, he rushed in to the warm and welcoming waves of the Pacific Ocean.

Slade didn't know it but he was being watched.

# Chapter One

'Bikinis!' announced Mitch Buchannon to the assembled members of the LA County Lifeguard Team who had assembled at the headquarters building.

Satisfied that he had caught their attention – or, at the very least, the attention of the male members – he continued:

'The next order of business is our policy on string bikinis!' he said.

'All those in favour say "aye",' joked Captain Ben Edwards, one of the lifeguards who had been working at Baywatch ever since Mitch could remember.

'Aye!' Every male member of the lifeguard team shouted as one.

Mitch glared at Ben. This was supposed to be serious stuff, he reminded him. At the start of every summer, Mitch always briefed both the new and old lifeguards on the safety regulations and rules down on the beach, and while string bikinis might not be the most important thing to bear in mind when you're out there in the ocean saving someone's life, at least Ben could set a good example to the others!

'The definition of buttocks is as follows,' said Mitch and read from a small notebook, trying hard to keep a straight face.

' "The protuberance at the rear of the human body from the uppermost cleavage of the nates – " '

A hand went up. 'What's a nate?' asked Matt Brody, the good-looking teenager who had recently joined the Baywatch rookie team, and was in training to become a fully-fledged lifeguard.

'These are nates!' said CJ, the impish blonde with a reputation for playfulness, and slapped him firmly on the behind.

Mitch smiled and continued: 'If you see any portion of skin on the beach fitting that description – '

'Contact Mitch immediately!' jeered Ben.

'No, it's a fifty dollar fine!' he replied, and slammed the rulebook shut. 'And now for my next announcement. I would like to announce that this will be my last announcement at our morning briefings! From now on, if you have any problems with scheduling, health insurance, or your love life, contact the new Supervising Lieutenant!'

'Hey, the County's finally sprung?' asked Newman, a balding moustachioed man who had been a good and loyal friend of Mitch for some years now.

He knew how frustrated Mitch had been recently, having to work as the acting Supervising Lieutenant. For Mitch, being a lifeguard meant working down on the beach, saving lives (and, sure, occasionally checking out the nates on some of the Californian girls there); it didn't mean pushing pieces of paper around an office, and making sure that the administrative side of the lifeguard operation ran as smoothly as possible.

'That's right,' Mitch said. 'They've finally come up with the money and appointed someone!'

'What beach is he from?' asked Ben.

Mitch shrugged. 'Your guess is as good as mine. All I do know is that the second he shows up my feet are back in the sand where they belong!'

He clapped his hands together and stood up, to indicate that the meeting was over.

'OK, everybody, that's it! Have a great day

and wear lots of sunblock – it's gonna be over a hundred degrees out there today!'

As the lifeguards hurried out of the meeting room, all eager to get down to the beach, Mitch called one of the younger trainee lifeguards over to him.

'Summer,' he said to the pretty blonde-haired rookie, 'you are going to stay in the office and observe how our headquarters runs with Ben. That guy knows more about lifeguarding than anyone I know.'

Summer's face fell slightly: she wasn't exactly thrilled by the idea of staying in the air-conditioned office all day when everyone else was out in the sun.

'Don't worry, Summer, I'm going to show you how to handle an octopus!' Ben declared grandly.

Matt Brody gave her a sympathetic pat on the shoulder as he made his way out. 'Have a good one!'

'Yeah, Matt, you too.'

Mitch walked up to the young dark-haired man. 'Matt, how'd you like to go surfing today?'

'You're kiddin' me, right?' Matt asked.

CJ sidled up to Matt. 'You *can* surf, can't you?' she teased.

'Hey, sure I can,' said Matt, wounded at the

playful slight to his masculine pride. 'It's one of the things I do the best!'

'You ever surfed Tequila Bay?'

Matt shook his head. He knew of the bay's reputation as one of the best spots to surf in the whole of Southern California; he also knew of its other reputation as the place where gangs of surfing sleaze-balls and dropouts often hung out.

'There are too many worms in that bottle,' he stated.

'Yeah, local worms who think they own the beach,' agreed Mitch. 'They put a couple of surfers from the valley in hospital yesterday . . .'

Matt looked interested: this sounded serious.

'Nobody's talking to any of the lifeguards,' Mitch said. 'So we thought maybe you could go and get us a couple of names.'

'Sure, why not?' said Matt, and Mitch smiled. He knew he'd been right to choose Matt.

Matt Brody liked to cultivate a 'bad guy' image, and at the times when he was roaring down Santa Monica Boulevard on his enormous motorbike, dressed only in jeans and a battered leather jacket he looked very much the part. But Mitch had guessed correctly that that was only a pose and that deep down Matt was a particularly sensitive and ultimately moral person.

'Just don't let them play pinocchio on your snout,' said CJ, tapping him on the nose with her fist. 'We leave in five minutes!'

*

The yellow scarab sped through the waters of the Pacific Ocean, bouncing along the waves like a pebble that had been flipped over a lake, and throwing up a spume of spray in its wake.

At the wheel was CJ, enjoying the feel of the wind as it blew her long blonde hair behind her. Sitting on the edge of the boat, dressed in a one-piece black surfing suit, was Matt. There was a small radio transmitter strapped to his belt. He was looking longingly – not at CJ, which was unusual because Matt particularly appreciated beautiful women – but at the steering wheel.

'When is it gonna be my turn to drive?' he pleaded like a young kid who wasn't being allowed to play with his big brother's favourite toy.

CJ turned to him, and gave him a superior, but not unkind, smile.

'If and when you make it out of rookie school!' she said, having to shout to make herself heard above the noise of the engine.

'C'mon, CJ, I've been racing these muscle boats since I was twelve!'

'And that was a really long time ago, wasn't it?' she said sarcastically. 'How old are you, Matt? Seventeen?'

Matt gave CJ the sort of look which would make any red-blooded female student at Malibu High go weak at the knees.

'How old are you?' he asked huskily.

'Old enough to separate the men from the boys!' she said. It was obvious that smouldering good looks didn't have the desired effect on every member of the female sex.

'Oh . . .' CJ's good-natured but pointed rebuff shut Matt up and they continued the rest of the journey in silence.

Finally CJ slowed the boat down, and indicated a small rocky promontory in the distance.

'That's Tequila Bay,' she said. 'I'm just going to pull around the point and drop you off.'

Slowly and carefully, she eased the boat up to the rocks, while Matt took out his surfboard and splashed it over the side into the water. He dived in after it, and began to belly-paddle around the promontory.

CJ called after him: 'Remember, Matt, you're still a rookie – you're not a lifeguard yet. At the first sign of trouble, activate your transmitter and I'll come and get you out!'

'*Pas de problème. Le trouble, je l'adore!*' he said.

'Huh?'

'French. I said that I can't wait for trouble!'

CJ watched thoughtfully after Matt as he paddled away from the boat and into the wilder surfing waters of Tequila Bay, where he would then be able to take advantage of the tide and stand up on the surfboard.

Like Mitch, who could see the real Matt beneath the façade, CJ decided that Matt was too headstrong for his own good, and sooner or later someone was going to teach him a nasty lesson. But he was also a mystery: they said that his father was a big novelist and screenwriter and lived up in the artists' colony in Malibu. So how come Matt spoke French? And not just a few words, but fluent and perfectly idiomatic French at that.

There was a lot more to Matt Brody, rookie lifeguard, than met the eye, CJ realised.

# Chapter Two

Jimmy Slade rode the crest of the wave like he was a natural part of it, seeming almost to fly through the air as the tide swept him and his surfboard up towards the shore of Tequila Bay. He felt the thrill of being at one with the ocean, the exhilarating touch of the wind on his face, and knew that he could never live the big-spending city life of his contemporaries. Who cared for money, for designer clothes, and careers, when you had a pair of swimtrunks, a surfboard and the whole Pacific Ocean as your playground?

On the shore, a group of young surfers in their twenties were watching Slade as he performed a switch foot, shifting his main body weight to one side so that he cut across the wave, and altered his direction. It was an impressive display of technique.

'Just who is that guy?' asked one of the girls in the group. 'He surfs like a real pro!'

Cuervo, her boyfriend, took a long drag on his cigarette and then threw it angrily onto the sand. He was a typical Californian beach bum: long dirty blonde hair and a body which had been toned and defined up at Muscle Beach, still firm and muscular, even though it was beginning to show the signs of too many bottles of Budweiser around his belly.

He said nothing, just sat there watching Slade, through narrowed jealous eyes, as the expert surfer weaved in and out of the currents. By his side, his girlfriend looked at him with a concerned expression on her face. Cuervo was silent, far too silent; and that was when he was at his most dangerous.

Out on the ocean, Slade had now been joined by another surfer who had come in from behind the rocky promontory which jutted out onto the Pacific.

Matt rode the waves with Slade, altering his direction when Slade did, always taking great care not to get too close and crash into him or cut across his path. Surfing might look simple, but it could be highly dangerous. A crash between two surfboards, and Matt might be in the position of having to use his newly-acquired lifeguarding skills much sooner than he thought.

From his vantage point on the beach, Cuervo watched as Slade and Matt sped to the shore. The two surfers were pretty good, he had to admit to himself, although Slade was plainly the more experienced of the two. He looked at his fellow surf bums, who were also observing Slade and Matt.

'Man, they are *awesome*,' breathed Beaver, a slightly-built young surfer with narrow eyes and a weaselish face.

'OK, they cut a good wave!' snarled Cuervo and walked angrily away.

Cuervo was an excellent surfer but those two guys out there might just be able to give him a run for his money. Beaver had touched on a raw nerve: it wasn't enough for Cuervo to be an above-average surfer, he had to be the best, the top dog.

*Too right they're good*, Cuervo brooded. *Too damn good, in fact . . .*

As Matt and Slade belly-boarded in, Matt introduced himself and complimented Slade on his surfing: he'd never seen anything like that since he'd watched the last televised world championships.

'Where d'you come from?' Slade asked.

'Hawaii,' joked Matt. 'I paddled the wrong way . . .' Matt didn't want to reveal who he was until he was sure that Slade wasn't one of the guys he'd come after. 'So what are you doing here?' he asked, slyly.

'I usually surf around here when there's nobody about,' said Slade. 'Some of the best waves for miles around here are in Tequila Bay!'

'Are you one of the Shooters?' Matt asked.

'Never heard of them,' said Slade after a slight pause.

Matt eyed him with suspicion. He wondered whether Slade really did know something or not. Mitch had said that no-one on the beach was willing to be forthcoming about the slime-balls who were ruining the waters for everyone else. Was Slade hiding something?

'They claim that they own these waves,' Matt remarked.

Jimmy Slade shrugged, and what he said next convinced Matt that, as far as the Shooters were concerned, he knew nothing.

'No way they can say that,' he stated simply. 'The waves belong to whoever's on them!'

He glanced back out at the water. The breakers were coming in even faster and higher now. 'Want another ride?' he asked.

'Too right!' said Matt and within minutes he

and Slade had paddled further out and had started riding the big waves.

As Matt went for a particularly high wave, a little way off from Slade, another surfer suddenly seemed to appear from out of nowhere, cutting across his path. Matt yelped and kneeled down on his board, struggling unsuccessfully to regain his balance. With a mighty *crash!* he fell into the water, while the current carried his surfboard to the beach. Thrashing about in the water, Matt saw Cuervo surfing in to land, laughing at his predicament. With a grunt of anger, he started to swim after him.

By the time Matt had reached the beach – followed by Slade, who had seen the whole thing – Cuervo had picked up the rookie's surfboard, which had been washed up by the tide, and was walking off with it.

Matt raced after him. 'Hey! That's my board!' he cried.

Cuervo turned and sneered. 'I don't know you,' he said, and signalled for his friends to join him. 'Get off *our* waves or we'll drown you.'

'*I'm* not done surfing yet,' said Slade who had come up to them. There was a dangerous tone in his voice.

'Look, we don't want any trouble,' Matt said reasonably. 'All I want is my surfboard back.'

'Finders keepers!' jeered Toke, another of Cuervo's surf buddies.

Slade saw red, and advanced threateningly on Toke, who lashed out at him with his own surfboard. Slade ducked just in time and then threw himself onto Toke, hitting him square in the face with his fist.

*Oh-oh, here come trouble!* thought Matt as Cuervo dropped his surfboard on the sand and approached him menacingly. He activated the transmitter on his belt, and then launched himself into the fight.

\*

On the scarab moored around the promontory, CJ picked up Matt's emergency signal. Immediately she picked up her own radio transmitter, and called headquarters.

'KMF 295 from Baywatch Rescue. I'm receiving an emergency transmission from Matt Brody!' she said urgently. 'Responding code three! Request immediate backup!'

\*

Cuervo's fist slammed into Matt's stomach, winding him and knocking him to the ground. The blond lost no time in taking full advantage of Matt's fall, and dived on top of the rookie, smashing another fist into Matt's face. Blood began to trickle down Matt's temple.

Together they tussled on the sand, first one gaining the upper hand and then the other. But the bigger man was stronger than Matt, and it took him all his strength to hold Cuervo off as his powerful hands reached for Matt's throat.

A few yards away Slade was pinned to the floor by Toke, who was rubbing his face in the sand. With an almighty heave, Slade pushed the surf bum off him, and leapt to his feet, crouched, and made ready to spring.

Suddenly a cry came from Beaver. He pointed to the open sea. 'Come on, guys, let's get out of here!'

Through dazed eyes, Matt looked in the direction Beaver was pointing. The scarab, piloted by Kelly, was already zooming through the water towards them. Following in its wake were two Baywatch lifeguards on power bikes, alerted by CJ's distress call.

Cuervo and Toke ran to grab their surfboards just as the power bikes reached the shore.

'You haven't seen the last of us,' he growled at Slade, as they ran off up the beach to their waiting truck. 'The next time we meet you, surf boy, you're going belly up, man!'

# Chapter Three

Much to Summer's disappointment, the 'octopus' Ben had promised he'd let her wrestle had proved not to be a killer monster up the beach at Redondo. No, this octopus was proving a much trickier customer to deal with.

Ben was instructing Summer how to operate the antiquated Baywatch telephone system. Wires criss-crossed the old machine, connecting into sockets which could transmit a call from one extension to another. She wished she was with CJ and Matt over at Tequila Bay; coping with this octopus made dealing with a few thugs down on the beach a piece of cake.

Ben looked out of the window to see the figure of a solitary woman standing on the balcony overlooking the beach. She was wearing a short-sleeved white shirt, which bore the badge

of the LA County Lifeguards' Department, and
a knee-length black lightweight skirt.

*Uh-oh*, thought Ben. *Trouble.*

*And trouble of the most unwelcome kind . . .*

'Summer,' he said. 'Get Mitch on the phone,
will you? He's down in the garage.'

Summer nodded, and looked at the maze of
wires and connections, wondering which one
would put her in contact with the garage.
Meanwhile, Ben stood up and walked out of the
office and onto the balcony.

'Stephanie?' he said.

The woman turned around. She was excep-
tionally pretty with long dark hair which had
been cut into a fringe and shone in the bright
Californian sunlight, and a beautiful porcelain-
doll face. The moment she saw Ben her face lit
up and she rushed forward to plant a kiss on
his cheek.

'Ben! How are you!'

Ben grinned. 'Hangin' on in here like a bar-
nacle, Stephanie,' he said. 'But just look at you!'

'At me?' Stephanie asked knowingly. 'Or at
my uniform?'

*The uniform of the new Supervising Lieuten-
ant of Baywatch*, Ben realised. *And we'd all
thought he was going to be a guy!*

Before Ben could reply, they heard someone
clattering up the steps which led to the balcony.

'Hi, Ben, Summer said that – ' Mitch began and then stopped dead in his tracks as he saw Stephanie.

To say that he was flabbergasted was like saying that the Pacific was a nice little paddling pool. Stephanie was absolutely the last person in the world Mitch Buchannon had ever expected to see again.

Ben discreetly withdrew back into the office.

Mitch and Stephanie stared at each other for several unbearably long seconds, neither of them quite knowing how to break the ice, ice which had been frozen solid now for three long hurting years.

Finally Stephanie took a deep breath. 'Hello, Mitch,' she said, and looked around at the beach and the ocean – anywhere, in fact, than at Mitch. 'Not much has changed around here in three years, I see – certainly not you.' She finally found the courage to look him in the face. 'You're still fluffed and buffed . . .'

Her voice tailed off and another awkward silence ensued.

Still Mitch didn't say anything, just continued to stare at Stephanie with narrowed, accusing eyes. Stephanie had been expecting this, had been dreading it, but it still didn't make it any easier.

'Look, Mitch, I know how awkward this is,'

she said. 'Believe me, if I knew that I was going to be transferred to Baywatch I never would have accepted this assignment.'

'It's not too late to change your mind,' Mitch finally said in a passionless monotone. And then he added bitterly: 'You're *very* good at that.'

Stephanie coloured. 'I worked hard for this promotion!' she claimed angrily.

'Do what you want,' said Mitch bitterly. 'I'm sure you will anyway.'

And with that, Mitch stormed off back down to the garage, leaving Stephanie standing alone on the balcony.

Ben, who had been observing Mitch and Stephanie's reunion from behind the office window, walked back out onto the balcony.

'It took him a long time to get over you, you know,' he said.

Stephanie nodded sadly.

Although Ben's voice was soft, and he still clearly liked Stephanie a lot, there was a touch of gentle recrimination in his voice. Without another word he turned and walked down the steps. Ben found Mitch in the Baywatch garage, angrily loading empty water drums into the back of a truck.

'You feel all right?' he asked sympathetically.

Mitch threw a final water drum noisily into the truck and turned back to his old friend.

'I feel like Humphrey Bogart in *Casablanca*!' he laughed bitterly. 'Of all the beaches in all the towns in all the world, she has to walk into mine!'

# Chapter Four

*Just like Humphrey Bogart in* Casablanca!
Mitch thought, as he pulled the truck off the
highway and onto the beach. *Old Bogie had
gotten his act together when Ingrid Bergman
had left him for someone else, hadn't he? Just
like me, in fact. And then years later – wham!
there she was back again, and the memories and
the recriminations and the yearning, they all
came flooding back!*

He looked out at the ocean, and he rubbed
his wet eyes with the back of his hand. It was
no use being angry, he realised, better to recall
the happier, better times. Mitch smiled, thinking of the good times he'd shared with Stephanie. Three long years ago . . .

'*You must remember this,*

*A kiss is still a kiss . . .'*
Three long, long years ago . . .

*

On a June day, three years ago, Mitch had staggered wearily into the locker room after a hard day's work at Baywatch. He'd stripped off his clothes and, dressed only in a short towel, walked into the empty showers.

Or rather, they should have been empty. Standing in front of him, with her back towards him, was a beautiful long-haired woman, totally unaware of his presence. As she towelled herself dry she hummed a song to herself. Mitch coughed loudly to announce his presence. The woman turned around. Although she instinctively raised a towel to cover the top half of her which was unclothed, she didn't betray any surprise; a cool head on a beautiful woman – Mitch liked that.

'Am I on the wrong side or are you?' she asked, at the same time admiring Mitch's firm well-built body.

'This is the men's locker room,' said Mitch. 'The women's locker room is on the other side.'

The pretty dark-haired woman raised her eyes heavenwards as if to say: *My God, what a klutz I must look!*

She gave an embarrassed grin, and reached out her hand for Mitch to shake.

'Sorry. I'm Stephanie Holden,' she introduced herself. 'I'm subbing for Jill while she's on vacation.'

Mitch shook Stephanie's hand and, as he did so, the towel which was wrapped around his waist fell to the floor. He hurriedly bent down to pick it up and to cover himself, as Stephanie Holden gazed on appreciatively.

'Well, I'm Mitch Buchannon,' he said. *All of me!* 'Welcome to Baywatch!'

'Thank you,' said Stephanie and smiled.

There was something very endearing about this hunky lifeguard, she thought. *Hey, if all the lifeguards around here are as hunky and good-looking as Mitch Buchannon, maybe I'm really gonna enjoy working as a temporary lifeguard at Baywatch this summer!*

\*

But Stephanie Holden never did get to meet any other hunky lifeguards that summer. *Or at least not in the way she'd intended*, thought Mitch, as he continued to gaze out at the ocean. He'd made sure of that. Within days they had officially become an 'item', and he and

Stephanie spent almost every waking hour together.

Mitch remembered with fondness their treks out into the countryside or the San Bernardino National Park to the east; he remembered the night they had dinner at the exclusive Spago's restaurant in Los Angeles (it had taken a hefty sum out of Mitch's monthly pay cheque but Stephanie had been worth it); or the day they took Hobie, his son from his previous marriage with whom Stephanie got on very well, on a no-expenses-spared trip to Disneyland.

He smiled as he recalled nights spent at his home with Stephanie, in front of a roaring fire, or intimate candlelit dinners *à deux* at the fancy Italian restaurant where Mitch knew the proprietor.

He remembered splashing about in the ocean with Stephanie like a couple of kids, giggling at the reactions of passers-by; or walking along the shore arm in arm and watching the sun go down over Baywatch, sinking deep down into the Pacific Ocean. But most of all Mitch remembered the feeling that here at last he might have found someone who could fill the empty gap in his life after his divorce had finally come through; that here at last was someone who could be his equal partner, in whom he could confide, who was great fun to be with, with whom he could lower his defences. Here at last was someone he could let himself fall in love with; someone whom he could trust.

Mitch smashed his fist angrily into his other hand, and frowned.

*What a prize jerk I showed myself to be!* he growled to himself. *Someone who loved me? Someone I could trust? Then why the hell did Stephanie Holden leave me, dump me like yesterday's newspapers? ... If she loved me like she said she did, why the hell did she leave me at the harbour, like a spotty kid being stood up on his first date?*

*Why has she never even tried to make contact with me for the past three years!*

\*

As Mitch was driving along the Pacific Coast Highway, Stephanie was unloading a large cardboard box stuffed full of papers and official files from her car. As she staggered up the steps and into the office of Baywatch headquarters several people asked if they could help her, but she turned down all their well-meant offers of assistance. Stephanie Holden was her own woman and she needed no help from anyone; besides, if she was to be in ultimate charge of the day-to-day running of Baywatch she had to

prove right from the very start that she didn't
have to rely on another living soul.

With a relieved gasp she dropped the heavy
box down onto the desk which had been
assigned to her and half the contents of the box
promptly spilled out in front of her. She waved
a hand at one of her fellow officers as if to say,
*Hey, no problem, I'm in charge now. Any chaos
around here – I'll handle it!*

She began pulling open the drawers of her
desk and indiscriminately throwing in her
papers and files: she could organise them later,
she thought; at the moment all that mattered
was that she had a clear workspace on which
to file her reports. As she opened one drawer,
she noticed lying inside it a polaroid snap of
Hobie, Mitch's son from his previous marriage.

Stephanie smiled – she'd always been very
fond of the tousle-haired young lad with his
cheeky grin – and realised that Mitch must
have been using this very same desk when he
was working as the acting Supervising
Lieutenant. He'd obviously not had time to
clear the desk of his personal possessions, she
realised; maybe she ought to wait until he got
back.

Curiosity got the better of Stephanie and she
rummaged through the contents of Mitch's
desk; after all, they'd once been lovers, privy to

each other's deepest secrets – surely he
wouldn't mind? But there was nothing of any
interest in the drawer, just a rag-bag selection
of official forms, paper clips, and pens. There
were a couple of receipts from some swanky
restaurants in downtown LA, and Stephanie
wondered idly just who Mitch had taken there.
Their reunion had been so swift and acrimoni-
ous that she hadn't had time to ask him if he
was currently seeing anyone.

Stephanie silently scolded herself. *Hey,
they'd been finished for three years now! Why
should she be bothered if Mitch had a new girlfriend or not? It wasn't like she was still carrying a torch for him, was it?*

Stephanie was about to close the drawer
when she noticed something lying inside which
brought the memories flooding back. It was a
narrow strip of multi-coloured cloth. It was
frayed and torn now, and the colours faded with
age and use, but she still remembered vividly
that night, three years ago, when she had given
it to Mitch . . .

*

. . . 'So what is it?' asked Mitch as Stephanie
tied the strip of cloth around his left wrist. They
were sitting by the fire in Mitch's apartment,

and a half-empty wine bottle was on the floor
beside them.

'It's a friendship bracelet,' she explained as
she tied the knot. 'You have to keep this on
your wrist now until it wears out and falls
off . . .'

'What? You mean *everywhere*?'

Stephanie nodded. 'That's right. In bed, in
the shower, in the ocean, on the beach. It's a
symbol of our feelings towards each other.'

Mitch made a mock-grimace as she tied it
tightly about his wrist. 'Well, just make sure
that you don't cut off my circulation!' he joked.

'According to a lot of the women I've met
down on the beach, I already have,' she said
only half-jokingly. 'And they're not at all happy
with it!'

Mitch grinned, and turned away embarrassed. 'What can I say?' he chuckled. 'What
can I say?'

He knew that ever since he'd been separated
and then divorced from his ex-wife, lots of the
girls on the beach had regarded him as a prize
catch. That was part of being a lifeguard, he
guessed: because you strut your stuff on the
beach all day, and you might even save somebody's life, everyone thought you were very
glamorous.

And what the hell! He'd enjoyed the adu-

lation (all of the lifeguards did if they were
honest with themselves), and sure, he'd fooled
around with a couple of them. But there'd been
nothing serious. Until now, that was.

Until Stephanie.

'You don't have to say anything!' Stephanie
laughed.

She knew of Mitch's reputation, and she also
knew how much he cared for her. She kissed
him on the lips, not the long deep kiss of lovers
who think that their new passionate romance
might not last but the kind of brief peck of
people who are sure in their love, who know
they don't have to prove anything to each other
any more.

'What are you thinking of?' she asked softly,
her lips close to his.

'I'm not thinking,' Mitch lied.

'Well, what would you be thinking about if
you were thinking?'

Mitch smiled; he couldn't fool Stephanie for a
second. And he suddenly decided that he didn't
want to.

'I'd be thinking that this whole thing has got
to be crazy because the ink on my divorce
papers is hardly dry . . .'

*Oh-oh, I've just gone and said the wrong
thing*, Mitch realised as Stephanie's face fell
with hurt and disappointment.

*But was there something else there as well?*
*Something she was holding back from him?*

Mitch reached out and held her hand, as if
to reassure her.

'Is this a ricochet romance?' she asked. 'Did
I get you on the rebound?'

'No.' Mitch's voice was firm, meaning it. Then
he smiled. 'No, you stole me at mid-court!'

Stephanie sighed with relief and the atmosphere between the two of them lightened up.

'Oh I did, did I?' she teased. 'Well, what am
I supposed to do with you now?'

Mitch pretended to consider the possibilities.
'You fancy some fancy dribbling and slam
dunk?'

'To win the game?' asked Stephanie, joining
in the spirit.

'No, to send in overtime!'

'Sounds interesting . . .'

'Wait till the playoffs this weekend,' said
Mitch. 'One on one in Catalina,' he said, referring to the island of Santa Catalina off the
south-western tip of Southern California.
'Come with me this weekend.'

Stephanie grew even more interested as
Mitch elaborated: 'The view of the harbour, the
balcony under the stars,' he enthused and
winked mischievously at her. 'First one to score
twenty wins!'

'You're on!' she said eagerly. 'But what about Hobie?'

She liked Hobie a lot but she hardly relished the idea of bringing him along on a romantic weekend away.

'No problem,' Mitch assured her. 'He'll be with his mom until Monday.'

Stephanie beamed and looked seductively at Mitch. 'So what about a practice game right now?' she suggested silkily.

Mitch needed no further encouragement. Lovingly they fell into each other's arms.

\*

*What a prize jerk I showed myself to be!* Stephanie berated herself angrily, *I was falling in love with one of the very best, and there I went and screwed it all up!*

*And not just for me, but for Mitch as well! I'm surprised he's even speaking to me!*

\*

*Damn Stephanie Holden, and damn her for coming back to Baywatch!* Mitch cursed as he watched the waves crash on the rocky shoreline. *Does she realise how much she made me feel a fool that day when we were supposed to go to Catalina?*

He closed his eyes and remembered.

It was a Saturday morning, and he'd arrived at the dock especially early to buy two tickets for him and Stephanie to catch the first morning ferry to take them over to the island.

He stood by the dock, dressed in a T-shirt and Chinos, the two tickets in his hand. Over his shoulder he'd slung an overnight bag.

He looked at his watch and frowned. Quarter past seven. Stephanie should have made it here by now: she was always so efficient, so punctual. He'd never yet known her to be late. Mitch shrugged. She'd probably been delayed in the traffic; she would be here any minute now.

Another quarter of an hour passed, and Mitch began to grow impatient. He was aware of other passengers making their way to the ferry, and staring at him curiously and at the two tickets in his hand. Some of them smiled sympathetically at him, as if they had already made up their minds about what had happened. Another quarter of an hour passed, and still there was no sign of Stephanie. The ferry blared out the all-aboard siren, and sailed away from the dock, leaving Mitch deserted, humiliated and heartbroken on the quayside.

And from that morning three years ago until

today, when she had turned up at Baywatch as Supervising Lieutenant, Mitch Buchannon had not seen or heard anything of Stephanie Holden.

*Damn her!* he said as he revved up the truck and drove angrily off down the road. *After what she did to me there is no way that Stephanie Holden and I are ever going to work together at Baywatch!*

# Chapter Five

Matt winced as CJ dabbed iodine onto the cut above his right eye in the sick bay at Baywatch headquarters. The young blonde tut-tutted sympathetically at his pain, but if Matt was looking for any similar sympathy from Garner, the burly black cop stationed at Baywatch, he was out of luck. With his arms folded, and a stern, disapproving look on his face, Garner looked down on Matt and Slade as he might have done at a couple of street kids, caught up in a local brawl down in West Hollywood.

'So the one guy almost decapitates you with a surfboard,' he said to Slade. 'Then what happened?'

'Then we go at it!' Slade said simply.

'Look, we gave you their descriptions,' said

Matt impatiently. 'Why don't you just go and bust them?'

'We can only get them on a charge of assault if they initiated the fight,' Garner pointed out matter-of-factly.

'We didn't start it,' Matt insisted, but Garner wasn't so easily convinced.

'Who threw the first punch?' he asked.

'Well, I guess I did,' said Slade and shrugged. 'You know, it's like the big wave's comin' and you want to get it before it gets you . . .'

'Garner, it was obviously self-defence!' CJ insisted, getting annoyed at what she regarded as nothing more than legal nit-picking.

'I'm sure it was,' he said. 'But the District Attorney's going to ask the same question.'

Matt sighed. He didn't fancy a grilling by the DA, especially when those scumballs deserved everything they got, and more besides. By his side Slade stood up and headed for the door.

'Look, man,' he said to Garner, 'there's a lot of risks in the ocean. If it's not those Shooters then it's something else . . . I'm out of here!'

He waved goodbye to CJ, and gave Matt a comradely slap of the hand.

'Wait a minute, Slade,' said Garner.

'What is it?'

'I'm going to need a phone number and an address where I can reach you.'

Slade grinned. 'No phone,' he said. 'The address is 853 DTS.'

'Is that a street?'

'No. It's a licence plate!' he explained and walked out of the surgery.

Matt smiled as he watched his new-found friend leave. He wished he had the same sort of freedom. Sure, it was great if your folks were rich like his and you lived in a fancy house in Malibu, and you sometimes even got to meet the big movie stars whose screenplays his dad wrote, but there were times when Matt longed for the opportunity to go where he wanted, and when he wanted.

'Don't worry, Garner,' he said, as Slade departed. 'You'll be able to find him wherever the surf is happening.'

\*

Summer stared at the ocean as she had done every day since she and her mother, Jackie, had arrived in Pittsburgh. From the very first moment in Southern California she had promised herself that she was going to learn how to surf if it was the last thing she did. After all, it was a sin to let all that ocean go to waste!

The beach was deserted except for a van, against which someone had leant a surfboard.

Checking that no one was around, Summer took the abandoned surfboard and laid it on the warm golden sand. She stood on the board and began to practise on the firm ground the moves she'd seen the real surfers do out there on the ocean waves.

From behind her she heard the sound of someone laughing and clapping. She spun around, an embarrassed look on her face.

'You should pull on the tube, or you're gonna get worked,' suggested Slade, who had been watching the pretty girl with a great deal of amusement.

Summer suddenly felt like a little girl again, caught trying on one of her mom's dresses, or pretending to be a rock 'n' roll singer miming to the latest Cher CD.

'I kind of always wanted to learn how to surf,' she admitted to the handsome newcomer.

'Maybe you should try it out in the water sometime?' Slade suggested helpfully.

Summer looked down at the surfboard and picked it up. 'Say, is this yours? I'm sorry – I hope I didn't do anything to it.'

Slade waved her concern aside: he might have got upset if he'd caught someone riding his board in the ocean, but he guessed a little pretend-surf on the sand wasn't going to harm it none.

David Hasselhoff as Mitch Buchannon.

Nicole Eggert stars as rookie lifeguard, Summer Quinn.

Alexandra Paul as Stephanie Holden and Pamela
Anderson as C.J. Parker.

International surfing champion, Kelly Slater, stars as
Jimmy Slade.

David Charvet as rookie lifeguard, Matt Brody.

Jeremy Jackson stars as Mitch's son, Hobie Buchannon.

Lifeguard Lieutenants Mitch Buchannon (David Hasselhoff) and Stephanie Holden (Alexandra Paul).

David Hasselhoff as Mitch Buchannon and Kelly Slater as
Jimmy Slade.

He noticed the Baywatch badge on the side of Summer's one-piece bathing suit. 'You a lifeguard?'

Summer nodded, and then corrected herself. 'Well, I've just made it through the qualifying swim,' she admitted. 'But rookie school doesn't start till next week. My name's Summer . . .'

Slade seemed amused by her name: whatever had happened to ordinary names like Brenda, or Sally, or Jane?

'The ultimate California girl,' he laughed.

'I wish! What's your name?'

'Slade . . .'

'Just Slade?'

'Jimmy,' he said. 'But everyone calls me Slade.' He held out his hand for her to shake. 'Nice to meet you, Summer.'

'Slade,' Summer began tentatively, 'would you teach me how to surf?'

Slade considered the pretty young girl from Pittsburgh, and the look of eager anticipation on her face. She really did want to learn how to ride the waves, he realised. He also realised just how attractive she was. What the hell! It could be fun!

'Sure,' he said and smiled. 'Why not?'

# Chapter Six

Mitch paced around his living room in irritation, his cordless phone rammed up to his ear. On the other end of the line was Chief Thorpe, his immediate boss. The Chief was trying to be reasonable with Mitch but the lifeguard was hearing nothing of it.

'This isn't just personal!' Mitch barked down the phone. 'If Stephanie Holden and myself can't work together' – and Mitch's tone suggested that they would never be able to – 'we'd disrupt the entire headquarters! Look, you're in charge now, and you can nominate anyone you want. And I'm telling you – it's either her or me!'

There was a knock at the front door. 'There's someone here now. I've got to go. The ball's in your court. But you know how I feel.'

Mitch switched the phone off and stalked over to the door. His face was red with anger and frustration. Stephanie had hurt him, and it was going to be a cold night in hell before he'd ever bring himself to try and understand her or even consider staying on the same planet as her.

He opened the front door.

'Hi, Mitch.'

*Uh-oh, I get the feeling that Hell's just frozen over . . .*

'Can I come in?' asked Stephanie.

For once Mitch was speechless. At Baywatch headquarters, dressed in her uniform of white blouse and smart black skirt, it had been easy to be annoyed with Stephanie. Now, dressed as she was in designer civilian clothes she suddenly seemed much less officious and threatening.

And Mitch remembered just why he had been so attracted to her.

'How's Hobie?' she asked casually, as Mitch invited her in. 'I'd love to see him.'

'He caught a summer cold,' said Mitch and nodded upstairs. 'He's sleeping.'

Stephanie looked around the room: everything was in the same place as it had always been, all just as she had remembered it. She might have been away only for a week instead of three long years. She noticed that all it lacked, in fact, was a woman's touch.

'So – are you dating anyone in particular?' she asked awkwardly.

Mitch didn't reply, just stared at her accusingly.

Stephanie returned his stare. *Don't you think it's hard for me as well?* she seemed to say.

'Why are you here?' Mitch demanded, in a voice laden with recriminations.

'I'm here because I know that it must be hard to have someone you practically trained end up as your boss!'

'You're not my boss!' said Mitch, rising to the bait. 'You are responsible for headquarters. *I'm* responsible for the beach!'

'That is not entirely accurate,' Stephanie corrected, suddenly the efficient administrator again, the one who always plays it by the rules. 'But the point is that I've invested too much in my career to walk away from this job . . .'

'I thought that was your style, to walk away,' Mitch said bitterly.

That hurt, but Stephanie knew better than to let it show. 'I'm sorry that I hurt you, Mitch,' she said, and meant it. Deep down, Mitch knew that she meant it too. 'Believe me, it was the only way . . .'

'There are a lot of other ways to end a

relationship besides standing up a guy by the ferry, and shoving a note under a door,' he said coldly.

*What did you take me for, Stephanie? Just another fling, just another diversion? Just another convenient way of filling in time during the summer? I thought we had something good going together for us, you and I! How wrong can you get!*

'I didn't want it to end, Mitch,' she said. *My God, I really didn't want to hurt you – you must see that!*

'Then why the hell did you leave me at the ferry?'

'It wouldn't have worked for us, Mitch,' Stephanie claimed, and her normally calm voice was shaking now. *Please, Mitch, you have to believe me!* 'I did what was best for both of us!'

Mitch shrugged with a nonchalance he certainly didn't feel.

'What difference does it make anyway?' he said. 'It's all water under the bridge now . . .' *God, you really cut me up when you left, you know that?*

An awkward silence followed with neither of them sure what to do next. Finally Stephanie said:

'Mitch, how long did you wear that friendship bracelet after I left?'

'What bracelet?' asked Mitch, knowing perfectly well what Stephanie was referring to.

'The one I tied on your wrist – over there by the fireplace . . .'

'Oh, *that* bracelet!' he said, pretending that he'd just remembered. 'I cut it off and threw it away the next day,' he lied.

'You cut it off?'

'Yeah. Snip, snip . . .'

Stephanie reached in to the pocket of her jacket, and pulled out the friendship bracelet she'd found in Mitch's desk drawer.

'What the hell were you doing going through my desk?' Mitch demanded angrily.

'The friendship bracelet's not cut, Mitch, it's worn through,' she pointed out, with a sad note of triumph in her voice.

Mitch turned his face away. 'So I snagged it on some rocks when I was going scuba diving,' he claimed unconvincingly.

'It must mean a lot to you if you kept it all those years . . .' she said softly.

'I threw it away in a junk drawer . . .'

Stephanie shook her head; there was no way she was going to get through Mitch's wounded masculine pride.

'Mitch, it's a *friendship* bracelet,' she said. 'I know we can never be lovers again, but can't we at least be friends?'

Another awkward silence followed in which Mitch tried to say something. But Stephanie had hurt him so hard all those years ago, he didn't want to fall into the same trap again.

Stephanie looked on, and understood.

Mitch had always been stubborn, and found it difficult to express what he really felt deep down. *Just like a man!* she thought wryly. It might take some time, but maybe they could still be friends again – if they both worked at it, if they were both prepared to give ground . . .

'Look, it's kind of late,' said Mitch. 'I don't want to wake up Hobie . . .'

Stephanie got the hint. She stood up and moved to the door, and was almost about to plant a goodnight kiss on Mitch's cheek when she thought better of it.

'Tell him hi for me,' she said. 'Goodnight, Mitch . . .'

'Goodnight, Stephanie . . .'

# Chapter Seven

The following morning, Summer got her mom, Jackie, to drive her down to Tequila Bay where she was due to meet Slade who had promised to teach her the rudiments of surfing.

'I sure hope I don't mess up,' said Summer, as Jackie turned off the highway.

'Why ever should you, honey?' Jackie asked, thinking her daughter was talking about rookie school.

Summer smiled. Her mom was only about sixteen years older than she was, and her best friend after all: she felt she could tell her.

'It's just that every time there's a cute guy around I can't seem to concentrate . . .'

'Well, honey,' said Jackie philosophically, 'that is a problem because Mitch is your boss . . .'

'*Mom!*' Summer reproved. 'Not Mitch! I'm talking about Jimmy!'

'Oh, Jimmy! Of course you were talking about Jimmy!' Jackie said quickly. 'Still, Mitch is pretty cute.' She paused and then added nonchalantly: 'Is he seeing anybody at the moment?'

'I don't know!' said Summer, and sighed. They'd been in Southern California not even a month yet and already her mother was trying to get her to match-make for her!

'Couldn't you find out for me, huh?'

'No way, Mom, no way!' Summer replied and laughed. Jackie stopped the car and Summer leapt out, kissing her mother on the cheek.

As Jackie drove away she looked in her rearview mirror at the figure of Jimmy Slade who was running up the beach to greet Summer.

*Not bad*, she decided, *not bad at all!* Summer seemed to have a knack for making friends with all the cutest and hunkiest guys on the beach. First Matt, and now Jimmy.

*Which all goes to prove she takes after her good ol' Mom*, thought Jackie with a grin, and drove back onto the highway to LA.

\*

Summer spent the rest of the morning listening

to Slade as he guided her patiently through the basics of surfing. With the surfboard on the sand he showed Kelly how to stand on the board with her feet apart, and how to bring weight to bear on one side of the board by leaning to the left or the right and so alter the direction in which the board was moving. She learnt how to drop to her knees on the board, in order to lower her centre of gravity and stay on the board when there was danger of losing her balance and falling into the water.

As Slade guided her step by step, it was obvious that surfing was his entire life. He had an encyclopaedic knowledge of the sport, and told her how it had probably originated in the Polynesian islands, and that Captain Cook was the first Westerner to describe the sport all the way back in 1771 on a trip to Tahiti. He described to her the thirty-foot high waves at Makaha Beach in Hawaii which he had ridden and which were supposedly the highest rideable waves anywhere in the world.

Summer was fascinated by his enthusiasm (and not a little by Jimmy Slade himself) and by mid-morning Slade had decided that she had learned enough to try her first ever surf in the Pacific Ocean.

Summer watched carefully as Slade belly-paddled out until he had reached deep water where he then grabbed the edges, or 'rails', of his board and, in one swift and fluid movement, heaved himself up into a standing position. Twisting his body this way and that, he manoeuvred his board into the waves.

'OK, Summer!' he called out. 'Now it's your turn!'

Summer bit her lip and followed Slade out into the ocean. When she was close by him she grabbed the rails of her board, and tried to stand up. The board wobbled precariously beneath her feet as she tried to steady it. Slowly she rose to her feet . . . and with a yell of surprise fell crashing back into the water. The force of her fall caught Slade off-balance and, with a laugh, he tumbled into the water too.

'OK,' he gasped as he rose to the surface. 'We try again. And again. And again until you get it right!'

Summer and Slade were enjoying themselves so much that neither of them noticed the slim figure of Beaver as he watched them from the coast.

*So*, the surf bum thought, *they've come back after we warned them off!* Her turned around and raced back up the beach. There was going to be a lot to tell Cuervo and the others.

# Chapter Eight

While Slade was teaching Summer the basic techniques of surfing, Mitch was enjoying his first full morning back down on the beach. It was good to be down there in the thick of things again, instead of at Baywatch headquarters, pushing pieces of paper round a desk and co-ordinating the rescue operations along their stretch of beach.

*Yeah*, thought Mitch, *there sure was nothing to beat the feel of the sand between your toes, the sun on your back and the salt-smell of the great Pacific Ocean.*

He belonged here, he realised, doing things, saving lives, not just organising the patrol and sending other people out on rescues. And that was, at least, one thing for which he had to be grateful to Stephanie, he thought. Now that she'd taken over as Supervising Lieutenant the beach was his own again.

It was still early morning but the beach was already packed with eager sun-worshippers, the dedicated surfers, and office workers determined to get in an early-morning swim before taking on the stresses of the day. To his left, a gaggle of chattering German tourists had already grabbed the best places on the beach and were excitedly laying out their towels and putting up their beach umbrellas. Mitch grimaced as he thought of the burns their white skins would suffer if they didn't put on enough sun block (which, like most tourists, they probably wouldn't). He was about to go over to them and give them a word of advice when he heard a cry from down by the shoreline.

'Hey! There's something wrong with that guy!'

'What guy?'

'He's in trouble!'

All thoughts of the German tourists forgotten, Mitch turned around in the direction of the cries and whipped his binoculars up to his eyes. There, in the middle of the ocean, a middle-aged man was thrashing around in the water, obviously in a great deal of difficulty.

'He's having a seizure!' someone cried.

'He's going to drown!'

There wasn't a second to spare. Left in the ocean for another minute the man would be dead. Mitch ripped off his red lifeguard's sweat-jacket, and raced down to the ocean and dived in. His arms and legs pumped and ached as he sped through the choppy seas like a fish, heading towards the drowning man.

Strapped behind his back was a red rescue can; the golden rule in life-saving is to avoid contact with a casualty if at all possible. In their blind panic they might just as easily drag you under the water with them when you're trying to save their life. It was much better to hand him the buoyant rescue can which would help him stay afloat until he calmed down.

As Mitch approach the man, he followed another of the cardinal rules of lifesaving and called out to him, announcing his presence. The last thing he wanted was for the man to panic, and give up hope, just as help was at hand.

But it was no use; the man was suffering a fit and was oblivious to everything around him. Mitch realised that in this instance the buoyancy aid was going to be of no use whatsoever. The casualty's head sank under the waves for a second time.

Mitch dived and headed towards the sinking man. He swam up to him and tried to grab him and pull him towards the surface. The man was thrashing about in the water, clearly terrified, and as is usual in such cases, not thinking straight. In his panic, he grabbed hold of Mitch and began to drag him under with him.

Mitch was suddenly aware of a pair of strong female arms taking hold of the man. With the extra help Mitch was able to overpower him and draw him up to the surface. He placed his arm around the man's neck and began to drag him into the shore, as Stephanie held the man still in the water, stopping him from thrashing about and endangering his life even further.

When they reached the beach an ambulance had already arrived, alerted by CJ who had been watching the whole rescue operation from her watchtower. As the man was loaded into the ambulance, Stephanie asked for a major incident report, the form which had to be filled in every time any of the Baywatch lifeguards had performed a rescue. She looked at Mitch: it was the first time they had seen each other since last night.

'Shall I fill it in, or will you?' she asked.

Mitch took the form from her. 'I'll do it,' he said gruffly, avoiding any eye contact with her.

Stephanie panted and tried to catch her breath. 'We worked together pretty well out there,' she said. 'We made a good lifesaving team . . .'

'You're a good lifeguard,' Mitch said reluctantly, still not looking at Stephanie.

'Do you want to put that in writing?' she said, suddenly deadly serious. 'Chief Thorpe's just informed me that in order to remain at Baywatch you have to give me a letter of endorsement.'

That was news to Mitch but he continued to occupy himself with filling in the form. But both he and Stephanie knew that the requirement of a letter of endorsement wasn't normal procedure.

Mitch realised that Thorpe had stipulated that purely for Mitch's benefit: the ball was now in his court – it was up to him whether his ex-lover would remain at Baywatch or not.

'This time I guess it's you who gets to decide whether I stay or leave,' said Stephanie.

Mitch looked up searchingly at her. 'A letter of endorsement requires you to state specific reasons,' he said. 'Before I give mine I want to know *yours*. Why didn't you come to Catalina? Why did you leave?'

Stephanie gritted her teeth. *Damn! Do I have to tell him! Can't he just leave it?*

She looked at Mitch and realised that there would never be any peace between them until he knew the truth of why she'd abandoned him three years ago. Besides, her career was on the

line too: if she didn't tell him she'd lose her job
for certain.

She took a deep breath. *OK, Mitch, you
wanted to know — so here goes . . .*

'Because I was married!'

Mitch was totally bowled over. He'd never
suspected anything of the sort. For once he was
completely at a loss for what to say.

'We'd been separated for two months when I
met you,' Stephanie confessed; and now it was
her turn to avoid Mitch's eyes. 'The night before
we were supposed to go to Catalina he came to
see me, and pleaded with me to come back and
give our marriage another try. I'd seen the pain
that you'd gone through with your divorce and
I figured that our marriage was worth saving.'

She sniffed as the memory proved too painful
for her. 'It turns out that I was wrong — we got
divorced a year ago . . .'

'You should have told me,' said Mitch. There
was no tone of recrimination in his voice now,
rather a willingness to help and sympathise
with the woman he had once loved.

Stephanie bit her lower lip. 'I know I should
have done,' she said. 'I just couldn't face you . . .
I wanted to call you, but the longer I waited
the harder it got . . . And then it was just too
late . . .'

She looked at Mitch, silently begging his forgiveness. Mitch fought against an almost irresistible urge to take Stephanie in his arms and comfort her, but he realised that that would be wrong, that it would reopen a whole lot of old aching wounds for both of them.

'I've got to get back to my tower,' he said abruptly, and turned to go.

As he walked up the beach Stephanie called him back: 'If you can't give me that letter of endorsement, Mitch, I'll understand. But I hope that at least one day you'll be able to forgive me . . .'

Without a word Mitch turned and walked back up the beach.

# Chapter Nine

'I should never have told you guys that guy had come back here,' said Beaver, as he sat on a rock in the shallow waters of Tequila Bay.

Toke looked up angrily at him. 'Well, you did – so shut up about it now!'

Beaver looked on nervously at Cuervo and Toke who were standing waist-high in the sea. They were uncoiling a long loop of rusty barbed wire, one end of which they had already attached to a large rock about ten metres away. As they pulled the wire taut they were careful that it was concealed from view, just a few inches above the surface level of the water.

'Barbed wire, man,' said Beaver. 'That could slice him up pretty bad.'

'That's the whole point!' Toke spat out the words.

'This is *our* beach, *our* water,' said Cuervo. 'If we don't defend it we're going to have jellyfish like him all over the place!'

Toke laughed sadistically. 'If that guy comes back here again, he's gonna be sharkmeat!'

\*

The next day Mitch was in the Baywatch headquarters early, after having taken an early-morning surf, before the beach and the water became too crowded with tourists. He went over and sat down at his desk and took out a piece of official stationery from his desk drawer. He'd thought long and hard about Stephanie's letter of endorsement and he'd finally reached a decision.

*And it hasn't been an easy one*, he reflected as he began to write.

He looked up as the door opened. Garner was looking at him with bemusement.

'Paperwork at this hour?' he asked.

Mitch smiled as Garner continued: 'What is it with you beach people? Why do you insist on waking up at this ungodly hour?'

'It's so you pavement people don't bother us,' Mitch joked.

'Well, you bother us too!' was Garner's

friendly response. 'Besides, this is way too early to take down some Tequila Shooters . . .'

Mitch looked up from his letter, interested. 'I thought you didn't have enough evidence to bust those surf punks?'

'I don't,' Garner said simply. 'But I figured you could help us get some' — he looked down at the letter Mitch was writing to Chief Thorpe — 'That is if you're not too busy pushing your pen.'

Mitch stood up. 'That can wait!' he said, slightly relieved that he could put off writing the letter which would seal Stephanie's fate at Baywatch. 'Let's go and get those punks!'

*

Slade grinned as he watched Summer try to stand upright on her surfboard. 'Just concentrate on everything I told you,' he called out to her. 'Just try and become part of the wave and you'll be fine.'

With a look of extreme concentration on her face, Summer grabbed the rails of her board and stood up. And suddenly she was surfing! She gave a little cheer of triumph as she leant to one side and the surfboard responded to the change in weight by moving in that direction. Slade was right: if you tried to imagine you

were a part of the wave itself, then it was easy,
about as easy as . . . falling off a surfboard, she
realised, as she lost her balance and tipped over
into the water. With a sheepish grin on her face
she waded back with the surfboard to Slade
who was waiting for her on the beach and
trying not to laugh.

Summer glared at him good-naturedly as if
to say: *You say a word, Jimmy Slade, and I'll
crack you over your head with your own surfboard*. Then she noticed Cuervo and Toke
coming towards them.

'Don't worry about them,' Slade said and
pushed her gently aside. 'They're after me . . .'

Cuervo swaggered threateningly up to Slade
who tensed, ready for anything.

'Man, like what is it with you?' asked Cuervo.
'You a real headcase or something? Or are you
just plain stupid?'

Summer stepped between Cuervo and Slade.

'I'm a Los Angeles County Lifeguard,' she
said. *Or at least I will be* . . . 'We don't want
any trouble round here, OK?'

'Then why do you come looking for it?' asked
Toke.

'We didn't,' said Summer calmly, looking the
thug straight in the eye. 'We came to surf, and
this is a public beach.'

'This is *our* beach!' claimed Cuervo angrily.

'You want a piece of me?' he asked Slade, and pointed out to the ocean. 'Let's take it out there, just the two of us,' he challenged. 'Let's see who can beat who at surfing back to the beach! Loser disappears and never shows his face here again!'

Slade looked suspiciously at Cuervo: he was up to something, of that he was sure. But a challenge was a challenge. He turned to Summer: he didn't want her getting mixed up in this mess. 'Take my van and get out of here, Summer.'

Summer shook her head. 'No way,' she said adamantly. 'I'm staying here as a witness!'

Toke sneered. 'Then watch what happens to your boyfriend!'

*He's not my boyfriend*, she thought. *Well, not yet anyway . . .*

Slade picked up his surfboard. 'Let's go,' he rapped, and started to belly-paddle in the water towards the surf.

Cuervo chuckled to himself and followed Slade. As Summer watched them go, Toke slipped away. It was time to make sure that the barbed wire was in position.

When they were far enough out, Slade and Cuervo stood on their boards, slotting expertly into the waves, and started surfing back to the shore. Slade glanced over at Cuervo. He had to admit that he was a good surfer who seemed to know the currents and riptides of Tequila Bay like the back of his hand.

Cuervo rode the wave in a straight line, heading for the shore. He looked over at Slade who was surfing off to his left. Suddenly Cuervo veered to the left in an apparent attempt to cut off Slade. Slade cut out to try and avoid a collision with his opponent – and hit the barbed wire. With a cry of surprise, Slade felt his surfboard fly out from under him, and he smashed into the waves – and right back into the rusty barbed wire. As he thrashed about in the water in agony he felt the coils of wire wrap around his body, and the more he struggled to get free the more deeply the rusty spikes dug into his skin.

On the shore, Summer cried out in alarm as she saw Slade fall off his board and Cuervo head off in the opposite direction. Without a moment's hesitation she grabbed her own board and belly-paddled out into the ocean. When she got far enough out, she slowly raised herself to her feet, and began surfing towards him. *God, don't let me be such a klutz and fall in the water now*! she cried silently, as she tried to remember everything Slade had taught her about manoeuvring her board.

As Summer surfed out to the rescue, Mitch

and Garner drove up on the beach. Seeing the
commotion in the ocean, Mitch raised his binoculars to his eyes. It took him less than a
second to assess the situation. He tossed the
binoculars to Garner in the driving seat.

'Get the scarab out here!' he ordered and
leapt out of the jeep as Garner raised headquarters on the radio.

Mitch raced towards the ocean and dived in,
using firm strong strokes to get out to Slade
and Summer as quickly as possible.

Summer had now dropped to her stomach
again and was carefully paddling her surfboard
up to Slade. His face was contorted in agony,
and the water around him was red with blood.
She reached out her hand to him.

'Don't come too close,' he groaned. 'It's sharp,
it's wrapped all around me . . .'

He struggled, but the barbed wire just
seemed to pull him under the water. Slade was
losing a lot of blood; the world was beginning
to spin sickeningly around him.

In a shower of spray, his limbs burning with
exertion, Mitch swam up to the pair. He grabbed at Slade, trying to keep him still. The less
Slade moved, the less blood he would lose, and
the less the filthy spikes would cut into his
skin.

'I can't get loose,' he said through gritted teeth.

'We'll get you out,' Mitch reassured him. 'Just hang on in there.'

The scarab, alerted by Garner's urgent SOS call, was already cutting a path through the water. Leaning over the prow, CJ tossed a pair of wire cutters into the water, and Summer began frantically cutting away at the barbed wire around Slade's bleeding body.

'Get a chopper out here!' ordered Mitch.

'There's already one on its way,' she cried.

Satisfied that Slade was no longer in any immediate danger, and that Summer had almost cut her way through Slade's barbed wire bonds, Mitch turned and swam back to the shore. As soon as he reached shallow waters he raced after Cuervo who had been watching the rescue from the beach. As Cuervo turned to run, Mitch threw himself at him and brought him thudding to the ground in a football tackle. The two struggled on the sand, but this time Cuervo was taking on a stronger and bigger man. Mitch slammed Cuervo's face down into the sand, and then turned him over to smash him hard in the face.

Mitch was almost enjoying beating the hell out of the sleazeball; Cuervo deserved it. Mitch's job was making the beach safe for

everyone; scum like Cuervo were only concerned with destroying it for everyone but
themselves. Finally he let up on Cuervo and
dragged him to his feet. There was blood
streaming from the thug's nose, and a vicious
cut above his right eye. For a moment, he
looked furiously at Mitch, defying him to call
in the cops to arrest him. But both of them
knew that he didn't have any hard evidence
with which to convict either Cuervo or his
fellow thugs.

Cuervo spat at Mitch. 'I'll see you around,
lifeguard,' he growled and staggered off up the
beach.

Mitch had made an enemy for life; but at
least he knew that the ocean was going to be
safe from scum like that. After the beating he'd
given him, he was sure Cuervo would never
come near Tequila Bay again.

# Chapter Ten

Stephanie tried to take a sneaky look over Mitch's shoulder as he worked at his desk in the office. He looked up, annoyed at her curiosity.

'Didn't I tell you to stay away from my desk?' he reminded her grumpily.

Stephanie pulled a face and raised her hands in a gesture of mock surrender.

'You did,' she began, and continued sarcastically: 'I suppose the real question is how far away?' She gestured to the far corner of the room. 'Over there? Or on some other planet?'

She indicated the letter which Mitch had just finished writing. 'Is that going to be a letter of endorsement – or rejection?' she asked, trying unsuccessfully to sound unconcerned. She realised that her entire career depended on what Mitch had put in his report to Chief

Thorpe. She tried to sneak a look at the letter, as Mitch marked it with an official rubber stamp.

'*Do you mind!*' he snapped.

'Run out of venom, have you?'

'I think it's only fair that you read this before I send it on to Chief Thorpe,' Mitch said and handed the letter over to Stephanie.

*I hope you realise now how much you hurt me all those years ago, Stephanie*, he thought. *It was hard writing that letter, lady. But then, it's no more than you deserve . . .*

'Go on, read it!'

Stephanie took the letter from Mitch's outstretched hand and began to read: ' "With regard to Lieutenant Stephanie Holden's permanent assignment to Baywatch headquarters, I find it impossible – " ' Stephanie frowned but read on. ' "I find it impossible not to endorse Lieutenant Holden wholeheartedly! She is one of the most talented and dedicated lifeguards I have ever worked with and will be a valuable addition to headquarters!" '

Stephanie beamed and she looked tenderly at Mitch. 'Oh, Mitch, thank you, thank you!'

Mitch nodded with embarrassment and returned to his paperwork. 'No problem,' he said. 'It's what you deserve.'

Then he looked up and half-smiled at Ste-

phanie; maybe they were no longer lovers, he
thought, but that didn't mean that they
couldn't be friends. 'And Stephanie – '

'Yes?'

'Welcome to Baywatch!'

'Thank you, Mitch!'

Mitch stood up. 'It's still early,' he said. 'You
want to come for a run?'

'I've got a million and one things to do,' she
said. 'I've still got to find a place to live and
I've got to get things organised for rookie school
next week . . . but sure, why not?'

*

'OK, you're in charge of headquarters,' Mitch
stated as they ran along the shoreline in the
early-morning mist. 'The beach is my responsibility entirely.'

'That's not exactly true, Mitch,' Stephanie
pointed out and stopped jogging. She didn't
want to start off on yet another bad foot on
their first day of working together but she felt
that Mitch should know what the status quo
was.

Mitch stopped in his tracks too, pretending
not to have heard what Stephanie had just said.
'And you're not my boss!' he stated even more
firmly.

'Well, I think that's a matter of definition,' she began.

'Stephanie – '

'Yes, Mitch?'

'Am I going to live to regret writing that letter?'

'No,' she said. 'Trust me.'

And when she saw that Mitch still had his doubts she remembered that film they'd enjoyed watching on late-night TV, the one where the hero's girlfriend comes back after a long absence.

' "Our problems won't amount to a hill of beans on this crazy beach",' she misquoted from *Casablanca*.

Mitch grinned. 'You know something, Lieutenant?' he asked, affecting Humphrey Bogart's much imitated drawl from the same film.

'What's that?'

'This could be the start of a beautiful friendship!'

And with that they raced each other back to Baywatch headquarters.

# Chapter Eleven

Dressed in a tight blue T-shirt which empha-
sised his pectoral muscles and a pair of baggy
beach shorts, Matt skipped lightly up the steps
which led to the terrace of his parents' luxury
house in the Malibu artists' colony.

It was still early, but Matt hadn't been able
to sleep. Today was the first day of the lifeguard
rookie school, the first step in the assessment
which would determine who would qualify as a
fully-fledged lifeguard this year.

And even if he hadn't been so restless, he still
wouldn't have been able to sleep. His father
had been out on the terrace since dawn that
morning clacking away on his noisy old-
fashioned typewriter. With the noise that piece
of antiquated old junk made it was a wonder

Aaron Brody hadn't woken up the rest of the neighbourhood by now.

Aaron looked up briefly to acknowledge his son's presence and then returned to his typing.

'What you writing, Dad?' asked Matt brightly. His dad just grunted and continued working.

'Dad, why don't you come out of the Stone Age and get a computer like all the other writers around here?' Matt asked.

That did it. Aaron Brody was usually a man it was hard to annoy, but like many successful artists he was very superstitious and didn't take kindly to anyone criticising his beloved typewriter.

'Ten novels and eighteen movies on this machine, Matt,' he snapped. 'I'm not about to abandon it now!'

And with that he returned to his work.

'Well, maybe I should have been born a machine,' Matt said darkly, under his breath. Why did his Dad never seem to have any time for him? For Aaron Brody it was work, work, work; there were days when it seemed he didn't even notice that his only son was alive, and living in the same house as him!

His mother, Vivian, who was reclining on a sun-lounger, sipping a glass of early-morning

Buck's Fizz, sat up and looked disapprovingly at Matt's shorts.

'Your father has told you not to ride your motorcycle wearing short pants,' she reminded him in her strong French accent.

Vivian had met Matt's father in France over eighteen years ago when he had been attending a film festival; it had been love at first sight and when they had married she had moved out to Malibu with him. Still proud of her French background she had raised her son to be bilingual.

'Maybe I'll get lucky,' Matt replied in French. 'Maybe I'll get lucky and they'll have to replace my legs with mechanical ones!'

*And maybe then you and Dad might notice me!* he thought miserably.

He picked up his motorcycle helmet from off the breakfast table and ran down to the huge winding driveway where the bike was parked.

With a final bitter look at his parents, too wrapped up in their own worlds for them to show him how much they cared, he angrily twisted the throttle and roared off down the highway which led to the beach.

*

When Matt reached the beach, Summer was

already down there practising her aerobic exercises while at the same time clutching firmly on to her red rescue can which all the lifeguards were instructed to carry with them at all times.

He leapt off the bike and ran down the beach. 'Loosen up with that thing, Summer,' he laughed. 'You're not gonna drown out here on the sand!'

Summer's face beamed when she saw Matt. 'I'm just so nervous, Matt,' she said. 'I've been looking everywhere for you!'

'Yeah, my father's on my case again,' said Matt. 'He says I never finish anything I start.' He took hold of Summer's rescue can. 'I swear that the day I graduate from rookie school I'm gonna take this rescue can and shove it right up – '

'Right up where, Matt?' she asked, amused.

'Right up his typewriter!'

Summer smiled and took the rescue can off him, giving him a sympathetic pat on the back. She knew how badly Matt wanted to graduate rookie school and become a real lifeguard; he wanted it almost as badly as she did, in fact. Maybe if Matt really made the grade, his parents would finally notice him. Summer was only glad that she didn't have the same problems with her mother. She and Jackie were good friends; people had even mistaken them for sisters more than once.

Matt waved as Clint, a beefy brown-haired teenager and another one of the lifeguard rookies, walked up to them. Matt and Clint had a not always friendly rivalry going on between them but Summer didn't care one bit for the bragging swollen-headed rookie.

'Congratulations on beating me in the qualifying swim last week, Matt,' Clint said, and actually meant it. 'But I don't think luck's gonna get you through this time, pal. If you want to be Rookie of the Year you're just gonna have to go through me.'

Matt laughed. 'You're such a tortoise in the water, Clint!' he scoffed. 'I'll swim right round you!'

Summer pointed to Mitch and Stephanie who were walking down to the shoreline where a large number of rookie lifeguards dressed in black trunks, or one-piece bathing costumes, had already congregated. They rushed down to join them.

While Mitch and Stephanie were checking over the list of the rookies pinned to Stephanie's clipboard, Mitch felt someone tugging at his shoulder. He turned to see the eager grinning face of Guido, the beach's very own Mexican con-merchant and supplier of everything from dodgy sun protection creams to hot dogs and Cokes. Mitch grinned: there were times when Guido could be a prize pain in the ass, like that time he sold a party of girls organic bikinis which promptly disintegrated in salt water, but he was harmless enough.

*That shirt*, thought Stephanie after she had been introduced to him, *is definitely something else! There should be a health warning slapped on it by the Surgeon General.* With its garish colours and tacky pattern Guido's shirt showed as much good taste and restraint as a Madonna video!

'How are you doing, Guido?' Mitch asked.

'I am going to swim for you!' Guido announced grandly and moved his arms in a breast-stroke motion, almost knocking the bemused Stephanie out of the way.

'I been all day and all night in the water practising. Just look at my body!' he said and curled his arm in an attempt to display his scrawny biceps and triceps. 'All those muscles, all in one place!'

*The muscles you've got, buster, are all in your head!* Stephanie laughed silently to herself, but had to admit there was something very endearing about him.

Mitch too couldn't help smirking. Guido's continuing desire to become a lifeguard was unlikely ever to be fulfilled. He gestured over to all the well-built and muscular rookie life-guards.

'Guido, I really appreciate your enthusiasm,' he said. 'But I've got a lot of guys . . .'

That didn't discourage Guido however.

'I have what it is you need, Mitch,' he declared. 'So use me – use me till I am all of me all used up!'

Mitch smiled, conceding a sort of defeat. He realised that if he didn't give Guido something to do on the Baywatch team he would continue to make his and Stephanie's life a misery until he did. He raised his hands in a gesture of mock surrender.

'OK, Guido, I give in,' he said.

'You gonna make me a lifeguard at Bay-watch?' Guido couldn't believe his luck.

'Not a lifeguard, Guido,' Mitch said hur-riedly. 'But I might need to use you in some other capacity. If you're interested, that is . . .'

Guido let out a whoop of joy. 'Am I interested? Does a lifeguard wear red shorts!' After Mitch had arranged to meet him later, he scuttled off across the beach, probably to attend to one of his more shady deals, Mitch guessed.

Stephanie blew a sharp toot on the whistle she wore on a chain around her neck, and the

lifeguard rookies all stood to attention. Matt
and Summer were in the front row.

'Good morning!' Mitch called out, and introduced Stephanie to the crowd. 'Welcome to
Rookie School! Last year 16,934 people were
able to go home from the beach because LA
County Lifeguards saved their lives.'

The crowd looked at each other: it was an
impressive number, even for one of the most
densely populated stretches of beach in the
world. But there were even more impressive
figures to come.

'The record for rescues in *one* day by *one*
lifeguard is seventy-eight! Someone's life may
depend on what you learn here today. So pay
attention!'

He called Stephanie forward, and she started
to read off a list of points from her clipboard.

'Every single thing you do from this moment
on will be observed and evaluated,' she
announced. 'If you fail a written examination
you will be dismissed.'

In the crowd, Summer gulped. She knew the
requirements to become a lifeguard were high,
but she didn't realise they'd be this tough!
*What, you're not even allowed to fail one test?*
She looked nervously up at Matt by her side
who gave her a reassuring and encouraging
smile.

'Those of you who are not dismissed – or don't quit – during the next two weeks of intense training will be drafted to work on various beaches. Whoever is voted Rookie of the Year will be able to select his – or her – own beach.'

Mitch stepped forward and took over. 'You'll be learning about lifesaving techniques, lifesaving equipment, CPR, mouth-to-mouth resuscitation, and first aid,' he explained. 'But what we can't teach you is responsibility.'

Suddenly he stopped and marched up to Summer who was giggling. 'Did I say something funny?' he asked sharply.

'Er, no, sir . . .' she said, suddenly embarrassed.

'It was my fault,' Matt admitted. 'I said something to her.'

'Then why don't you share it with the rest of us?' demanded Stephanie, in the sort of tone usually employed by stern schoolmistresses on tiresome pupils.

Matt grinned. 'I was just wondering which of you would be my partner in mouth-to-mouth . . .'

There was a general snigger among the rest of the rookies which was instantly silenced by a frosty glare from Stephanie.

'Mr Brody, mouth-to-mouth resuscitation is *not* kissing!' she snapped. 'A lifeguard may have to give mouth-to-mouth resuscitation to a 250-pound truck driver, or to a two-year-old child. It is not a situation where one chooses a partner. This is not the dating game! Do I make myself clear!'

*Oh brother, has she ever put me in my place!* thought Matt.

'Er, yes, ma'am, that's perfectly clear,' he said sheepishly.

Mitch looked on worriedly. Stephanie was a great lifeguard, one of the very best, but there were times when she took her job a little too seriously. The kid had only been having a joke after all. He was probably as nervous as hell, and was just trying to ease the tension; he remembered that he certainly was on his first day of rookie school.

Stephanie could be the tenderest person ever – he knew that – but as soon as she put on her official uniform she seemed to forget all that. If she wasn't careful, Mitch decided, she'd make an enemy in Matt Brody.

'Good,' said Stephanie. 'Well then if that's settled it's time to move on to the Gauntlet!'

# Chapter Twelve

The Gauntlet was the ultimate test of any lifeguard, trying their courage, their strength,
their athleticism, their tenacity and their
swimming skills. They said that if you could
complete and survive the Baywatch Gauntlet,
you were top material, maybe even Olympic
standard.

But if you failed, then you might as well
give up any hope of becoming a Californian
lifeguard. Both Mitch and Stephanie had done
the test in their rookie days and even today
they could still remember the sheer terror they
experienced completing it, and the way their
limbs ached for days after.

Mitch gathered everyone around him down
at the water's edge and explained to the expect-
ant rookies just what the Gauntlet was.

'The Gauntlet is a lifeguard obstacle course,' he explained. 'You will run it twice. The first time is just for fun, to get the feel of it. The second time will be at the completion of rookie school. It will be the ultimate pass or fail test. Come through it and you might make a lifeguard; fail, and you can forget it!'

He drew everyone's attention to a row of floating red buoys which had been placed about a hundred metres out in the Pacific, and explained the course of the obstacle race. The rookies had to swim out to the buoys and tow one of them back to the shore; although they bobbed about quite happily on the surface of the water Mitch warned the rookies that they were much more heavy than they looked. After they had done that, they had to run for about half a mile along the shoreline before plunging back into the water and making for one of the high piers which dotted the shore. Ropes had been hung from the struts of the pier, and the rookies were required to climb up them to the top. From there they had to sprint to the end of the pier, and dive off back into the ocean, before swimming back to shore and running the final half-mile back to Mitch and Stephanie at the finishing post.

It was a harrowing prospect for anyone, especially a bunch of seventeen and eighteen

year olds who never had experienced anything
so gruelling before. But as Mitch told them, it
sorted the wheat from the chaff, the excellent
from the merely good. If you didn't think you
could do it, he told them, then you weren't fit
to be a lifeguard at Baywatch or any of the
beaches along the Southern Californian coast.

Everyone looked nervously at each other as
Stephanie put them on their marks.

'On your marks . . .'

Matt glanced over at Summer and smiled.
Although this wasn't, strictly speaking, a race,
the young girl from Pittsburgh remembered
what one of the female lifeguards had said to
her when she was attempting to qualify for a
place in the school. *Pace yourself: don't use all
your strength right at the start. Let the ones in
front of you tire themselves out first.*

'Get set . . .'

Clint stared straight ahead at the bobbing
buoys waiting for him in the ocean. His main
objective was to finish the Gauntlet in the first
half dozen or so – and give Matt Brody a run
for his money.

'Go!'

Stephanie fired her starting pistol and the
rookies, as one, dived into the ocean, frantically
cutting through the water. Matt and Clint were
in the lead as the saltwater stung their eyes

and within minutes they had each grabbed hold of one of the lines attached to the buoys and were beginning to drag them into shore.

Summer stayed in the rear, knowing that she'd need all her energy for the sprint along the beach to the pier. She was right: as she splashed out of the water, towing a buoy behind her, a rookie who had been way ahead of her in the water stumbled, exhausted: she'd already tired herself out by trying to swim too fast to the buoys. Summer guessed that she wouldn't be graduating from rookie school this year.

Summer's legs ached and her panting breath cut her throat like a knife as she ran across the beach. She never knew a half-mile could be so long: it seemed to take forever. The ground burned her bare feet, and she stumbled more than once on the shifting sands, where the waves washed up on the shore.

*Shoot!* she exclaimed to herself, as she tripped and picked herself up. Matt and Clint were now way ahead of her, and she was trailing behind.

*Take it steady!* she kept telling herself, as she felt herself panic. *This time round it doesn't matter who comes first or who comes last! It's completing the course that matters! Only that!*

Finally, after what seemed like hours, but had in fact only been a matter of minutes, she

reached the end of the run, and, without paus-
ing even a half-instant, dived into the shallow
water and made for the pier. Her hands reached
out of the water and grasped the end of the
knotted length of rope suspended from the
creaking wooden struts of the pier. With every
muscle in her body aching, she hauled herself
up out of the water and began to clamber up
the rope. The rope blistered her hands, tearing
the skin off them, and the rope swayed menacingly to and fro.

*Don't look down, just don't look down!* she
recited to herself over and over like a magic
charm. Summer was terrified of heights and
she knew that if she glanced down for even a
second she would freeze. Above her, many of
the others had reached the pier and were
already jumping off the end, like so many lem-
mings, back into the ocean. With a final grunt
of exertion Summer reached the top of pier and
pulled herself over the edge. This was the final
lap now, and her heart leapt with joy and relief.

She was going to do it! She was actually
going to complete the Gauntlet!

She ran to the edge of the pier. And then
froze.

Down below her, the waters of the Pacific
churned and crashed around the pier's stan-

chions. Summer felt dizzy. It was a long way down – such a long, long way down.

People who had been trailing behind her passed by, throwing themselves off the edge and into the water below. They were having no trouble, Summer realised. If they could do it, then so could she.

*Don't dive*, she reminded herself. *Just jump in feet first. There's no danger at all. If there is they wouldn't have made this part of the test.*

She prepared to jump.

And looked once more at the water, so very far away.

Summer shook her head, and tears came to her eyes.

*I can't do it! I can't do it!*

Resigned, she turned around and walked back down the length of the pier to the beach.

\*

As Summer tramped dejectedly along the beach back to the point where all the other rookies – *all the ones who hadn't chickened out*, she thought – were waiting, she heard someone call her name.

'It's Summer, isn't it?' asked CJ.

Summer remembered that it had been CJ who had given her the useful piece of advice

about pacing yourself in a race. *And a fat lot
of good that does you if you're a coward and
scared of heights like I am!*

'I guess everyone's going to know who I am
now,' she said morosely. 'The only one who
didn't make the pier jump!'

Summer began to move off but CJ reached
out and gently held her back.

'Hey, listen,' she said sympathetically.
'You're not the first rookie to be terrified up
there, and you definitely won't be the last!'

Summer shrugged diffidently. 'Well, what
difference does it make, anyway?' she asked. 'If
I don't make the jump in the real Gauntlet run
then I won't graduate from rookie school!'

'You'll make the jump,' CJ assured her.

'That's easy for you to say,' she retorted. 'You
don't know what it's like to look down at the
water and – '

'Feel like it's a hundred miles away?' CJ
smiled kindly. 'Your heart's beating so loud
that you can't even hear the waves crashing
below. Summer, I was the only one in *my* rookie
class who couldn't make the pier jump the first
time round!'

Summer's eyes widened. She'd heard that CJ
was one of the best lifeguards around.

'So how did you finally do it?' she asked,
intrigued.

'I decided that I wanted it more than I was afraid of it,' CJ replied. 'And when that final jump came, you know what I did?'

'No. . . . what?'

'I just imagined that there was somebody down there who was going to drown if I didn't. So I jumped . . . Think about it Summer, think about it . . .'

# Chapter Thirteen

Stephanie was bushed. It had been a hard day, what with organising the Gauntlet Run and then getting into the swing of her new office. Still, it was nice to have a place of her own to come home to.

She'd found the small beach house earlier that morning. It was in a great location, just across from the beach. It was spacious and, best of all, she could afford it all on her own!

It was going to be fun living by herself again, after sharing with roommates. At long last there'd be no one to criticise or antagonise her, no one to borrow her clothes or eat her food. She'd been lucky, but then there seemed to be a surplus of empty affordable apartments near the beach at the moment. CJ had told her that she too had found herself a new place.

Stephanie lay back on the sofa and switched on a classical station on the radio. She closed her eyes, yawned luxuriously, and relaxed. Suddenly someone turned the lock and opened the door. Stephanie jumped out of her reverie as CJ walked in through the door. CJ was as surprised as Stephanie to see her boss lying there.

'CJ! What are you doing here?' Stephanie demanded. 'How did you get the keys to my apartment?'

'*Your* apartment?' CJ asked, confused.

'Yeah.'

'Wait a minute, I rented this apartment from an old boyfriend of mine,' CJ started. 'His name's Mark – '

'Harris?' Stephanie completed the name for her, and CJ nodded. She had a very worrying feeling about all this . . .

'You know him?'

'Know him?' said Stephanie. 'I used to date him! He rented this apartment to me last week!'

*That two-timing good-for-nothing louse!* they both thought.

CJ stood back and folded her arms in a gesture of defiance. 'Well, I gave him first and last two weeks ago,' she claimed.

Stephanie stood up from the sofa, and folded her arms in the same defiant manner.

'So?'

'So I leased the apartment before you did!'

'Well, I'm here and I've taken possession,' Stephanie stated snootily. 'And possession is nine-tenths of the law!'

'Oh yeah?' said CJ. 'Well, if you want to get technical, consider this possession.'

She dragged a big suitcase into the apartment, and placed her foot on it triumphantly, like a mountaineer who's just climbed Mount Everest and is claiming it for his own country.

Stephanie and CJ had each just acquired an unwilling roommate.

*

By the following week things still hadn't improved. Stephanie, as the older of the two women, was much more practical and tidy, liking everything to be in its place. CJ, on the other hand, was a much freer spirit, with her head located for much of the time somewhere high up in the clouds where, in Stephanie's opinion, only another air-head could ever find it.

Stephanie, too, wanted to concentrate on organising and devising the tests – both written and practical – for the rookie lifeguards; and that was difficult to do when most of CJ's free time (at least when she wasn't leaving her dirty washing on the bathroom floor, or forgetting to put the top back on the toothpaste tube) seemed to be spent meditating.

Meditating for Stephanie meant an hour spent in silent and peaceful contemplation, perhaps listening to a favourite piece by Brahms or Mahler on the radio; for CJ it seemed to mean chanting out monosyllabic mantras at the top of her voice.

Finally it all got too much one night when Stephanie was preparing a meal and CJ waltzed into the kitchen and knocked into Stephanie, causing her to spill a load of salt into her mixing bowl.

'Look what you made me do!' Stephanie screamed.

CJ was shocked when she saw the amount of salt that had been spilt. 'You shouldn't be using salt!' she reproved.

'I happen to like salt!' *And what business is it of yours anyway?*

'It makes you bloat,' CJ claimed.

'Do I look bloated to you?'

CJ smiled; after all, she'd just finished her meditation. 'I'm in too serene a stage to engage in a bloat debate right now,' she said skilfully stepping aside the issue.

'You realise that this isn't working, don't

you?' said Stephanie angrily. 'We've been involuntary roommates for two weeks now . . .'

CJ shrugged as if to say *So what? I don't see any problem*, and opened a packed of quick-use macrobiotic rice.

'And I'm starting to break out into hives!' Stephanie exploded.

'Well, maybe its because you don't eat right,' CJ suggested and offered her some carrot juice from the refrigerator.

'No thank you,' Stephanie said frostily. 'I can hardly bear to watch you drink it!'

CJ shook her head sympathetically. 'Stephanie, your system is polluted,' she said. 'You should at least chant with me . . .'

'I don't want to chant with you!' Stephanie snapped. What she really wanted to do was hit CJ over the head with a good old-fashioned greasy frying pan.

Instead she said: 'And I certainly don't want to keep picking up after you,' and picked a cardigan off a kitchen chair which CJ had dumped there the previous night.

'So why do you keep on doing it?' CJ asked, not unreasonably.

'Because I hate wet clothes draped over chairs and doors to dry,' she replied. 'There's a new invention out, CJ. It's called a laundromat! Washers! Dryers! Why don't you use them?'

'Do you know what dryers do?' asked CJ. 'Dryers send out all sorts of bad elements into the air. Not to mention the waste of electricity. You know, I have a great book on saving the environment – I think you should read it.'

'How about one on saving my sanity first of all?' said Stephanie, and, conceding defeat, stormed out of the kitchen.

'Salt causes hypertension too, you know,' CJ called after her, as the kitchen door slammed shut.

She shook her head and tut-tutted to herself.

Really, Stephanie should learn to chill out and relax a bit more. She shouldn't take life so seriously. After all, it wasn't like this was the East Coast, or something. This was Southern California and being laid back was a major fact of life out here.

If Stephanie didn't wise up to that fast there was no telling what trouble she might cause down at Baywatch . . .

# Chapter Fourteen

' "Then move to the victim's head," ' Matt quoted the following morning, as he paced around his parents' terrace, trying to remember the correct procedure for mouth-to-mouth resuscitation.

' "Check the airway, take a deep breath, seal off the nose and deliver two long inhalations, one to one-and-a-half seconds in duration. Then move back to the chest, locate proper hand position and begin fifteen cardiac compressions." '

At the breakfast table, Summer slammed shut the text book and whistled in admiration. 'How did you learn this word for word?' she asked, clearly impressed.

'I guess I just have one of those memories,' he said.

Summer shook her head: she never realised

that learning how to become a lifeguard involved so much studying.

'You want a drink?' he asked.

'Yeah, give me one of those smart drinks and make it a double,' she quipped and reopened the text book. 'I think I'm gonna need it!'

As Matt went off to the kitchen to make her a drink, Summer was aware of someone staring at her. She looked up to see an older man, who looked remarkably like Matt, coming across the lawn.

'I'm Aaron Brody, Matthew's father,' he introduced himself, and climbed up onto the balcony where he sat down at the breakfast table. 'And you are?'

'Summer Quinn,' she said and shook Brody's offered hand. 'Pleased to meet you, sir.'

'Summer,' Brody repeated 'What an *enchanting* name . . . And why does a beautiful lady like you want to become a lifeguard?'

'Well, Mr Brody . . .'

'Please. Call me Aaron.'

'Well, lifeguarding is something I think I would be good at. And I really need the money.'

Brody arched an eyebrow in interest. 'Do you live alone then?' he asked. 'Do you support yourself?'

*What is this?* thought Summer. *Twenty questions?*

'No, I live with my mom,' she explained. 'We just moved out here from Pittsburgh. We've always been a, you know, two-income family.'

'So your parents are divorced,' said Brody and Summer had the curious sensation that Matt's father was actually taking mental notes of everything she was telling him.

'That's awful,' he continued although Summer wasn't convinced that he actually meant it. 'What happened?'

*Dad, knock it off!'* said Matt who had just returned with the drinks. He looked at Summer. 'Don't answer him, Summer!'

'Matt, I think your dad was just trying to be polite,' Summer said, attempting to defuse what was obviously a potentially explosive situation.

Matt shot his father a rueful look before turning back to Summer. 'No, he's just trying to probe you for material,' he said. 'Everyone he meets is just research for one of his novels or scripts.'

At the table Brody just smiled giving nothing away. 'Just lay off my friends, OK?' Matt snapped.

Brody chuckled. 'My son Matthew is uncomfortable with honest dialogue . . .'

Father and son stared at each other, each one

challenging the other to make some remark. Finally Summer broke the awkward silence.

'Look, Matt, I think we maybe ought to be going to the pool,' she said and looked pointedly at her watch. 'We're going to be late for the demonstration.'

'You go on ahead, Summer,' said Matt, still staring defiantly at his father. 'I'll catch up with you.'

As Summer stood up to go, Brody said, 'Don't get too attached to my son. He has a problem with commitment.'

*And if I do* thought Matt viciously, *then it's a case of like father like son, isn't it? Just keep away from my friends!*

'It was a pleasure to meet you, Summer,' Brody called as Summer skipped down the steps of the balcony, and made her way across the lawn and down to the beach.

\*

Stephanie felt her way underwater carefully, slowly, exploring every inch, every nook and cranny of the pool bottom. The special darkened goggles she was wearing ensured that she might as well have been swimming in pitch blackness, for all that she could see. All she had to rely on was her sense of touch, and the instincts that any trained lifeguard has to develop quickly in order to survive.

As she swam through the water, creating currents, she listened carefully for any change in the sounds echoing through the water. A simple change in the frequency of sound waves, practically unnoticeable even to the most trained ear, would indicate the presence on the bottom of the bag she'd been asked to locate and bring to the surface.

Through the darkened goggles she could make out the dim shape which Mitch had dropped into the pool earlier that day. With a strong flick of her legs she propelled herself towards it and grabbed it, and, in one swift, continuous movement rose to the surface of the pool.

As she broke the surface the assembled rookies, including Summer, burst into applause. Not only had Stephanie found the bag, she'd also stayed underwater for almost three minutes!

If anyone had had any doubts about Stephanie's suitability for the post of Supervising Lieutenant of Baywatch they were well and truly quashed now: Stephanie had just proved herself to be one of the best lifeguards Baywatch had seen in a long time. Mitch's letter of recommendation to Chief Thorpe had been no mean boast.

Stephanie pulled herself out of the water and removed the special glasses, and Mitch congratulated her on her performance before turning back to the rookies.

'That demonstration was to show you what it's like when a killer riptide turns the bottom of the ocean into a sandstorm,' he said. 'Sometimes you can't even see the submerged victim.'

'Now here's a question: what would you do in a rescue under a pier if a wave was about to slam you and your victim up against the piling?'

Clint, Matt's big-headed friend, knew the answer to that one.

'I'd put my body between the victim and the piling,' he said confidently.

Mitch smiled: the rookies always got that one wrong.

'Wrong!' he said. 'You should put the victim *between* you and the piling. Because if you, the lifeguard, get hurt you both might drown.'

He looked over to Stephanie, indicating that it was her turn to speak now that she'd caught her breath back. She held up one of the red buoyant rescue cans which all the lifeguards of Baywatch carried around with them, either in their hands or slung over their shoulders.

'This is your life's blood, both on the beach and in the ocean,' she declared importantly.

'Take it with you everywhere. When you swim out to a victim you must offer them the can first — it'll help them to keep afloat.

'However, if the victim approaches you he might be panicking. He could very easily pull you down under with him. Then you must use the rescue can to block and parry him.'

Stephanie stopped as she heard the roar of a motorbike. She looked over to see Matt leaping off his bike and racing down to the pool, tearing off his T-shirt as he approached, until by the time he reached Stephanie he was wearing only his beach shorts. A muttering came up from the crowd; everyone knew how strict Lieutenant Holden was on punctuality: Matt was bound to be for it now!

'I'm sorry,' he said and took his place in the line.

'Is that what you'd say if you were late for a rescue and somebody drowned?' demanded Stephanie angrily.

'*Si vous etiez en danger je vous sauverai avec plaisir . . .*' he said, hoping at least to charm a smile out of the Supervising Lieutenant.

But Lieutenant Stephanie Holden was made of much sterner stuff than the girls Matt used to impress with his fluent French down on Malibu beach.

'I understand French, Mister Brody,' she said

icily, making it quite clear that she wasn't in the slightest bit amused by his saying that he certainly wouldn't miss out on saving her if she was in danger. 'Get in the pool!' she ordered.

'Huh?'

'I said get in the pool!'

Matt shrugged his shoulders and leapt into the pool, hoping to redeem his reputation by showing to Stephanie that he at the very least remembered always to jump feet-first into any unknown waters. Stephanie, however, took not the slightest notice of him and addressed the other rookies instead.

'There's not one of you, man or woman, who I can't totally dominate in the water,' she claimed and the tone in her voice didn't encourage anyone to deny it.

'There's not one of you who could threaten my life with more strength, because I know how to protect myself – and the life of my victim.' She walked up the the edge of the pool, and looked at Matt who was treading water.

'All right, Mister Brody,' she said casually. 'Rescue me.' And Stephanie jumped, feet-first, into the pool.

In a shower of spray, Matt shot through the water towards Stephanie. Within seconds he had reached her and grabbed hold of her. As soon as he had done it he cursed himself. He'd already forgotten one of the main rules of life-saving: never come into contact with the victim if it's at all possible.

Stephanie had expected him to make that natural mistake, and smiled inwardly to herself. If she was going to pretend to be a drowning victim, then she was going to pretend to be a terrified and panic-stricken one as well. She clutched at Matt's neck, attempting to drag him down with her to the bottom of the pool. When Matt succeeded in shaking her off, she grabbed fiercely at his hair, making his eyes water. No matter which way Matt twisted and turned to avoid Stephanie, she somehow managed to retain her grasp on him, holding him in an underwater version of a half-Nelson. For all her slim and feminine physique Stephanie had a grip of iron, and Matt found it impossible to escape from her.

The water churned all about them, making it difficult to see, as Stephanie held Matt down on the very bottom of the pool. Matt's vision blurred as he began to find it difficult to breathe. Finally, when she thought he had had enough, Stephanie released her grip on Matt and he kicked himself up towards the surface, where he emerged blue in the face, and greedily gulping for air.

Stephanie followed him up at a pointedly

slower pace, and when she reached the surface she hardly gasped for breath at all. She was the first out of the pool, and she bent down to help Matt out, who angrily refused her help. In the crowd of spectators a few rookies (Clint included) snickered at Stephanie's humiliation of Matt.

'Learn these lessons here and now, before your and your victim's life are on the line,' Stephanie announced. 'If that had been a real incident we both could have been drowned by now.'

She cast a look back at Matt and gave him a gloating smile, as if to say: *That showed you, didn't it, big boy?*

'Thank you for illustrating my point so well, Mister Brody.'

Matt glowered at her. Here was something that he sure wasn't going to forget in a hurry. His folks ignored him all the time, and when he tried to get his act together and achieve something, people like Stephanie Holden always knocked him down again.

'You were a little rough on him, Stephanie,' Mitch remarked to her after he had dismissed the rookies for the day.

Stephanie shrugged, not caring. 'Mitch, our job here is to weed out the ones who don't have what it takes,' she said stonily.

'It's also to help the ones who have what it takes but don't know it yet!' Mitch reminded her equally stonily, and walked off to the locker room.

In the men's locker room, Matt was just towelling his hair and getting ready to leave. Mitch pulled him aside.

'You know something, Matt, you have everything in you to become a great lifeguard . . .' he began.

'How the hell do you know what I have inside of me?' the younger man countered angrily.

'Because when you run you let it out of you, when you swim you let it out of you,' said Mitch. 'Matt, you have got the potential in you of beating every other rookie in the school . . .'

'She made a fool of me out there in the pool!' Matt cried.

*She makes fools out of lots of people*, Mitch thought bitterly, *and I should know. But she doesn't mean it: that's only her way, and she regrets it later. But don't I wish that she would change her way!*

'Don't let Lieutenant Holden beat up on you, Matt,' Mitch urged.

'Lieutenant Holden!' Matt scoffed. 'Apparently she knows everything, right?'

'You could learn a lot from her,' Mitch reminded him.

'Yeah,' said Matt. 'I just did out there. I learned that I didn't want to be a lifeguard any more!'

Matt picked up his towel and stormed out of the locker room.

*Damn Stephanie!* thought Mitch. *What's she gone and done now?*

# Chapter Fifteen

The last day of rookie school finally dawned. Of the scores of rookies who had qualified, only about twenty or so now remained. The others had dropped out, realising that they'd never make lifeguard material, or had failed one of the written or practical tests.

Today was make-or-break day and as Stephanie looked around the room at the eager faces of the young would-be lifeguards she noticed that Matt was missing. For a moment she regretted the hard way she'd treated him the previous day, and then cast any self-recriminations or doubt aside. Lifeguards were supposed to be made of sterner stuff, and if Matt couldn't take the pressure, well, then, that was tough but there was nothing she could do about it.

There was something else she noticed as well. The communications room in which they were holding their final meeting had been apparently refurnished. The dull wooden chairs were now shining with polish, and even the dusty old blackboard was as if new, without a trace of chalk dust on its matt black surface.

'Who authorised the purchase of a new blackboard, and desks, and chairs?' she demanded, and the rookies laughed, the tension relaxed slightly. 'What's going on here?'

Guido came through the door, an enormous smile on his tiny Mexican face which almost – but not quite – outshone the brilliance of his latest Hawaian shirt.

'It's not new!' he crowed. 'I take the old and I make it look like new! I spent all day and all night, working and polishing, working and polishing and cleaning, and cleaning and polishing and polishing and cleaning.' He beamed at Stephanie. 'Just to make it look beautiful for you!'

Stephanie was touched, in spite of herself, and found herself turning red with embarrassment as Guido planted two enormous kisses on her cheeks.

'Why, thank you, Guido.'

'Ah, the pleasure, she is all mine!' claimed the little man.

'Well, er, keep up the good work, Guido,' she said and turned back to the class. They were all grinning at Guido who was obviously becoming besotted with their steely taskmaster.

'Congratulations to all of those who have made it to this last day of rookie school,' she said. 'Your last test will be the Gauntlet – and this time it's going to be for real.'

In the class Summer's face fell, as the nightmare of the previous Gauntlet returned to her. She knew that if she couldn't make the jump this time, her chances of ever becoming a lifeguard would be finished forever.

'It will be harder than the first time you ran it,' Stephanie continued. 'The dummies will be heavier, and further out in the water. This time the run will be longer and the pier jump higher.'

A worried murmur arose from the class as everyone looked nervously at each other. The first Gauntlet had been the mother of all tests to get through. Surely the real test couldn't be any worse?

Stephanie smiled, the genuine smile of the stern teacher who had put her students through all their paces, but also had an absolute confidence in their abilities.

'But I know you can do it!' she reiterated.

'You've worked really hard these past two weeks. Really hard. So go out and get them!'

The rookies filed out of the communications room and began to make their way down to the beach. Stephanie watched them go.

*Just don't let me down,* she said to herself. *Just don't let me down. Prove to me that I was right to have faith in you. Show me that all that hard work I put you all through was worth it.*

If Summer, or any of the other rookies, could have heard what Stephanie was thinking she would have been surprised. Stephanie genuinely liked the rookies – in the past two weeks she'd shown them a lot and they'd been through a lot together – but in uniform she always came across as the stern and demanding taskmaster.

But Summer had more important things to worry about. Echoing through and through her mind, taunting her and challenging her, she could hear Stephanie's words:

*This time the run will be longer, and the pier jump higher . . . the pier jump higher . . . higher . . . higher . . . higher . . .*

# Chapter Sixteen

'May I help you?' asked Vivian Brody politely as Mitch walked up the driveway to the Brody household. She noticed that Mitch looked uncomfortable in these wealthy surroundings, as if he wasn't used to such ostentatious displays of riches. Obviously, a friend of her son's she thought: Matt was always making friends with questionable people.

'I'm looking for Matt Brody,' Mitch said after he had introduced himself.

'That makes two of us,' said Aaron Brody as he came out of the house, smoking a big cigar. 'Matthew didn't come home last night.'

As Vivian invited Mitch to join them on the terrace Mitch realised that neither Brody nor his wife really cared where Matt was. As far as Mitch knew, he was their only son: surely they

should have at least shown some signs of concern when he hadn't returned home last night?
Instead, Brody was treating the whole affair as
though it was one great and crashing bore.

'You probably know that he's attending
rookie school,' said Mitch and was relieved to
see that Aaron and Vivian at least knew that
small but important detail of their son's life.

'Well, he had a little problem with one of our
other lieutenants yesterday and it seems that
he's run off . . .'

Aaron yawned and returned to the crossword
of the newspaper he was carrying.

'Matthew has a difficult time with authority,'
remarked Vivian and she poured Mitch a glass
of freshly-squeezed orange juice from a crystal
pitcher. 'He's a very sensitive boy.'

'I think Matt – Matthew – needs to accept
responsibility for himself and his own
behaviour,' Mitch countered.

Vivian looked interested. No one had talked
to her about her son like this before. 'And you
believe that becoming a lifeguard will help him
develop that?'

Mitch nodded. 'When you're responsible for
the safety of thousands of people on the beach,
then you *have* to be responsible.'

Brody gave a wry chuckle. 'And if you're

incapable of responsibility you'd be putting those people's lives at danger,' he pointed out.

'Mister Brody, I believe in Matt,' Mitch stated firmly.

*Which is more than you, as his father, seem to do!* he thought. *When was the last time you gave him any encouragement, helped him have faith in himself?*

'Given half a chance I think Matt can start believing in himself,' Mitch continued. 'Do you have any idea where I might find him? I sure would like to talk to him.'

'Probably off getting himself into trouble somewhere,' said Aaron blithely and continued his crossword.

*Damn you! Don't you care at all what your son gets up to?*

'He may have gone surfing,' said Vivian. 'His board and bike were missing this morning.'

'Thank you,' said Mitch as politely as he could manage, and returned to his truck in the driveway, leaving the glass of freshly-squeezed orange juice untouched.

*

Mitch almost missed Matt. As he pulled up on the beach at Tequila Bay, thankfully now free of Cuervo and his cronies, the rookie was dragging his surfboard out of the water. He'd been surfing for over an hour now, and he was panting with exhaustion and exhilaration.

*Hell, who needed the hassle of being a lifeguard, when you could have all of this?* Matt tried to convince himself. *Slade's got it right, all right. Just you, the surfboard, and the sea. All the fun and being responsible to no-one but yourself! Way to go, man, way to go!*

He turned round and saw Mitch racing across the beach towards him.

'Matt, wait up!' Mitch cried. Matt was already tying his surfboard to the back of his motorbike, and getting ready to leave.

'How did you find me?' asked Matt, when Mitch caught up with him.

'I just came from your home,' said Mitch. 'I had a little talk with your parents . . .'

Matt lowered his eyes to the ground. 'My father sure gives new meaning to the phrase family man, doesn't he?' he said bitterly.

'He thinks you're a quitter,' Mitch said.

Matt raised his eyes, and looked Mitch defiantly in the face, unsuccessfully trying to pretend that he didn't care in the slightest what his father thought of him.

'And what do *you* think?' he asked.

'I think you're afraid to win.'

Mitch stared back at Matt. *Go on*, his eyes seemed to be saying. *Go and prove me wrong!*

'I'm not scared of anything!' Matt protested.

'Then show me,' Mitch challenged. 'Show your dad. Show *yourself!*'

An awkward silence followed and Matt looked at Mitch strangely. No one had ever shown such an interest in him before, certainly not his parents.

'Why is my being a lifeguard so important to you?' he asked.

'Because you remind me of a young hothead I once knew,' said Mitch. 'Someone else who also had a big problem with his dad . . .'

'Eddie Kramer?' Matt said, remembering the young full-time lifeguard he had once met briefly, and who had now left Los Angeles to live in Australia with his new bride, Shauni.

Mitch smiled at the memory of Eddie and Shauni. 'No, this one was about a foot taller . . .'

*And got to be Lieutenant at Baywatch!* he thought.

'The Gauntlet starts in one hour, Matt,' he said. 'With you – or without you.'

# Chapter Seventeen

Mitch surveyed the assembled rookies on the beach. There was still no sign of Matt. He sighed; maybe he'd been wrong after all, he thought, maybe Matt just didn't have what it takes . . .

'OK, today you're on the Gauntlet – and it's against the clock,' he announced briskly. 'There'll be a staggered start. Two minutes between each group.'

Everyone looked apprehensively at the floating buoys, much farther out than they had been on the dummy run; at the running track flanked by LA County Lifeguard officials and now one mile long instead of just half-a-mile; and at the pier in the distance, twice as high as the first one.

Stephanie walked up to Mitch. There was something wrong, she could see that.

'Are you OK, Mitch?' she asked.

Mitch looked at his watch and then up at the boardwalk. *'Dammit!'* he cursed under his breath. He had to face it: Matt wasn't going to turn up. Mitch had tried his best, and it hadn't been good enough.

'All right, Stephanie, go ahead!'

'OK, group one, to the starting line!' Stephanie commanded.

A group of about ten very nervous rookies shuffled to the starting line. Stephanie fired her starting pistol and, with a roar, they were off.

She was organising the second group – which included Summer and Clint – when she heard the roar of a motorbike on the boardwalk. Everyone looked up, but it was only Mitch who allowed himself a quiet whoop of triumph. Still wearing his motorbike helmet, Matt was running down to the beach. There was less than a minute to go before the second group was due to set off.

He skidded to a halt in the sand in front of Stephanie, and took off his helmet.

I'm sorry I'm late, Lieutenant Holden', he panted. 'It will never happen again!'

'Join group two,' Stephanie said, trying not to smile.

'Thank you.'

As Matt joined the group, Clint cursed his luck. He'd been hoping that Matt wouldn't turn up. Matt was his only serious competition; with him out of the running he knew that he'd easily win the race.

Matt took off his T-shirt and grinned at Summer, and made the 'good luck' sign with his thumb and forefinger.

*Crack!* Stephanie fired her starting pistol, and the group raced off into the ocean. Clint and Matt were neck-and-neck as they swam for the buoys, but Summer kept behind, once again conserving most of her energies for the latter part of the race.

Constantly in her mind, as she dragged the buoy to shore, as she ran along the beach, as she swam back out to the pier, still ringing in her head like a bell of doom, were Stephanie's words: *This time the pier jump will be higher!*

*Maybe this time I'll be braver, maybe this time I'll do it*, she repeated over and over to herself. But deep down in her heart she remained unconvinced.

Finally she was standing on the edge of the pier. She looked down: it was time to face her fear. Below her the waters frothed and churned, splashing against the wooden stanchions. The lapping waves seemed to be laughing at her.

She shook her head.

She couldn't do it. No matter what. No matter that it meant being called a coward. No matter that it meant losing the chance of becoming a lifeguard at Baywatch. Summer simply could not jump off the pier into the water twenty metres below.

All around her, the other rookies passed her by and jumped into the water. They had no problems with it; or perhaps it was just that they didn't show their fear.

'Jump!' a voice shouted from down below. Summer looked over in the direction of the voice; CJ was watching her from the beach, urging her on.

*What was it CJ had said?* Summer asked herself. *Just pretend that there's someone drowning down there who needs your help . . .*

She bent her knees, and prepared to dive off the end of the pier. Looking down once again, she felt dizzy. It was such a long, long way down. *I can't do it! I can't do it!*

'Summer, jump!' Matt was at her side. 'Everyone's passing you! *Jump!*

Summer shook her head despairingly. 'No . . . no . . . no . . . I can't . . . don't make me . . . I can't . . .'

'Yes, you can!' barked Matt. 'Come on!'

Clint caught up with them, and jeered at

Matt and Summer. 'What's the matter, Brody? Can't make it?' He looked over at Summer. 'Just need an excuse to lose, huh?'

Matt ignored his opponent, even when Clint jumped over the pier, executing an elaborate text-book dive into the water. Summer looked down at the foam left in the wake of Clint's dive into the water. *No, not dived: crashed, hit, slammed into.*

'Leave me, Matt,' she cried. 'Don't let him win! You could beat him!'

Matt looked after Clint: he wanted more than anything in the world to teach Clint a lesson and to beat that arrogant, swell-head son of a bitch. And suddenly he realised that there was something much more important than his own dreams of glory and revenge. Summer was quaking like a leaf on the edge of the pier, too scared to move.

'I'm not jumping without you, Summer!' he insisted.

'Go, Matt,' Summer pleaded. 'If I can't do this by myself then I don't deserve to make it!'

Matt grabbed her hand. 'We'll do it together,' he said firmly. 'We'll jump together, OK?'

Summer looked uncertain.

'OK?' he repeated. Summer bit her lip and nodded weakly.

'One . . .'

She held Matt's hand more tightly.

'Two . . .'

Summer shut her eyes: *please, God, let it be over soon . . .*

'Three!'

Together Matt and Summer jumped off the pier, plummeting through the air like two stones down into the water some twenty metres below where they landed with an enormous *splash!*

It was one of the most terrifying – and happiest – moments of Summer's life as she surfaced, gasping not for breath, but with elation, and realised that she'd finally conquered her greatest fear. By her side, his dark hair plastered to his forehead, Matt grinned. He'd done it; no, they'd done it! He'd had the confidence in Summer's abilities, and he'd finally made himself responsible for another human being; it was a turning-point in both their lives.

Summer tried to breathe her thanks, but words weren't enough. Instead she turned in the water and pointed to the rapidly departing figure of Clint, swimming back to the shore and the final stretch of the Gauntlet.

'Now go and get Clint!' she shouted. 'Go, Matt, go!'

Matt pushed himself away from the pier and, with his lungs bursting, broke into a crawl, pushing himself to the limit to catch up with his rival. Summer followed a few metres behind. Up ahead, Clint cast a wary look behind him to see Matt coming up on him fast. He cursed to himself; there was no way he was going to let the rich kid beat him this time!

As soon as he reached the shallows, Clint splashed out of the water and headed off down the beach, running along the marked one-mile stretch back to the finishing line. Close behind him, Matt climbed out of the water, straining all his muscles to catch up.

But this time he wasn't just doing it for himself; he wasn't even doing it to impress the girls on the beach, or to make his folks sit up and notice him for a change. Matt Brody was running the race of his life for two people: Mitch Buchannon and Summer Quinn. Mitch and Summer had been the first people to show any faith or confidence in him for a long time. They both had said that he could win this race. And he wasn't going to let them down now!

Through eyes glazed over with sweat he squinted at the finishing line. It was only fifteen metres away now. And Clint was still in front of him!

Ignoring the pain in his legs, and his breath which ripped into his lungs like a rusted old knife, Matt increased his speed.

Ten metres.

Matt was almost neck-and-neck with Clint now. Clint glanced behind him, losing a valuable half-second.

Five metres.

Matt screwed his eyes shut, summoning every last ounce of strength in his body. His bare feet pounded painfully in the sand, and every step seemed to send powerful shock waves throughout his entire nervous system.

With a cry of joy as much as of pain, Matt Brody crossed over the finish line just two seconds in front of Clint.

# Epilogue

Eighteen extremely nervous young people sat chattering to each other in the main meeting room of Baywatch headquarters, each one of them oozing with about as much confidence as the average person in a dentist's waiting room. The door opened and Mitch and Stephanie marched in. Stephanie was holding a clipboard; each and every one of them – Matt, Clint, Summer and the others – knew that what was written on the sheet of paper attached to Stephanie's clipboard would decide their future as lifeguards once and for all.

'OK, listen up!' said Mitch and called the meeting to order. 'Both myself and Lieutenant Holden here know that you're anxious to hear where you'll be working this summer.

'But as you know there are eighteen of you

– and there are only thirteen positions open.
The selections, therefore, were based on com-
petitive results, test scores – and attitude.'

By Summer's side, Matt knew immediately
that he hadn't been assigned a place. If anything was going to be marked according to
attitude then he was a dead-cert loser every
time.

Stephanie stood forward. 'The assignments
this year are as follows . . .' She recited a long
list of names and the beaches to which they
would be assigned. As each person's name was
called out that person breathed a sigh of relief.

'And for duty on Baywatch itself,' Stephanie
concluded, 'Lewiston, and Summer Quinn.'

Summer gasped in disbelief. She'd made it!
Even her screw-up on the pier hadn't harmed
her score. She'd made it as an actual, real-life,
honest-to-goodness-mom-no-kidding lifeguard!
Matt patted her on the back and congratulated
her, but there was a disappointed look on his
face at being passed over.

'Lieutenant Buchannon will now announce
the name of the Rookie of the Year.'

'Of the six of you remaining,' said Mitch, and
looked at the six who included Matt and Clint,
'I'm sorry but five will have to wait for next
summer. But I'd like to thank everyone here

for making this possibly the best rookie school in LA County Lifeguard history.'

*Cut the crap*, thought Clint. *Let us know who's the best lifeguard among us!* It was obvious who Clint thought was entitled to that title.

'As you all know, tradition states that the Rookie of the Year gets his – or her – own choice of where they work. This year the choice goes to' – Mitch paused for effect – 'Matthew Brody!'

'Matt, I'm so pleased,' said Summer and hugged him. Clint scowled and left the room.

*What? Who? Me?* Matt couldn't believe it as Mitch walked up and congratulated him. *I thought you said that this thing is based on your attitude. My folks have always said I've a real bad attitude . . . Hey, I guess maybe they were wrong . . .*

'Congratulations, Matt,' smiled Stephanie. 'I always knew that you had it in you.'

*And you know something else?* thought Matt. *She means it!*

He turned to Mitch with a dazed look on his face. 'Why me?' he asked.

'Your unselfish support of Summer on the pier showed us a lot,' Mitch revealed. 'It's what lifeguarding is all about. Being there for each other, backing each other up . . .'

'Yeah,' agreed Matt, and looked meaningfully at Mitch. 'I've learnt that . . .'

'So which beach would you like to represent?' asked Mitch.

Matt didn't have to think. 'Well, if it's OK with you, I'd like to work at Baywatch.'

Mitch slapped him on the back. 'You've got it!'

'Thank you.'

'Your apprenticeship starts tomorrow,' said Stephanie and added mischievously: 'And don't be late this time, OK?'

'I'll be here early,' Matt promised.

'Just be on time, Matt, just be on time!'

\*

Guido looked solemn and more than little guilty as he turned up at Baywatch headquarters the next morning. Mitch had demanded that Guido be there at nine o'clock sharp and, in Guido's experience, nine o'clock appointments usually meant that someone was querying the existence of, if not his immigration and residence papers, then at least his permit to sell his dubious merchandise down on the beach.

Stephanie was waiting with Mitch when Guido turned up at the arranged time. She

looked reluctantly down at Guido's shirt which
was even gaudier than usual, and decided that
if the Mexican was going to insist on wearing
any more of his technicolor creations then the
least that she could do would be to invest in a
good pair of extra-powerful dark glasses.

Mitch looked up sternly at Guido from behind
his desk. 'Guido, Lieutenant Holden and I have
agreed that in the light of all the unauthorised
things you've been doing around here . . .'

'*Without* our knowledge,' Stephanie added
darkly.

'That you will be charged with – '

Guido gulped. This was it, he decided. Ten
years in the State penitentiary at the very
least . . .

Mitch smiled and corrected himself. 'That
you will be *in charge of* all the maintenance
duties on the beach. That is if you still want to
be our *official* maintenance engineer . . .'

Guido couldn't believe his luck. At last he
was going to be an official member of the Baywatch team!

'Engineer!' Guido cooed the word as though
it was the most beautiful sound in any lan-
guage. 'Oh, the responsibility! Do you think I
have it?'

Mitch nodded: even if Guido didn't, it would
keep his mind off some of his more questionable

enterprises. Guido turned to Stephanie, arms opened to embrace her. Stephanie beat a hasty retreat behind Mitch's desk.

'I . . . er, think you'll be quite sufficient, Guido,' she said. 'Congratulations!'

'Oh an engineer,' Guido said. 'The responsibility that lies on my shoulders! The challenge! The glamour!'

Mitch chuckled. He had a strange feeling that he was going to regret appointing Guido as the official Baywatch engineer. But there was no doubt that he'd liven the place up no end.

As would all the new members of the Baywatch team and their friends, he realised with a smile. Matt and Summer, CJ and Jimmy Slade, who was recovering now in hospital and would be back on the waves in no time.

And, of course, Stephanie. There were going to be some major disagreements between Stephanie and himself, not to mention between Stephanie and her roommate. And, if Mitch had allowed himself to be honest with himself, he would have had to admit that he was actually looking forward to them.

Yes, whatever else happened, Baywatch was never going to be the same again!

Join the **BAYWATCHERS FAN NETWORK** now and keep in touch with your favourite Baywatch stars and all the latest Baywatch news.

For further information please send a large s.a.e. to:

**BAYWATCHERS FAN NETWORK**
**PO BOX 1443**
**POOLE**
**DORSET**
**BH15 3YP**

## HOW TO ORDER YOUR BOXTREE TV NOVELISATIONS

**BAYWATCH**

☐ 1–85283–847–7 *The Devil's Mouth* £2.99

**BEVERLY HILLS, 90210**

☐ 1–85283–671–7 *The French Rival* £2.99
☐ 1–85283–680–6 *Beginnings* £2.99
☐ 1–85283–748–9 *No Secrets* £2.99
☐ 1–85283–749–7 *Which Way to the Beach?* £2.99
☐ 1–85283–820–5 *Fantasies* £2.99
☐ 1–85283–825–6 *'Tis the Season* £2.99
☐ 1–85283–816–7 *Two Hearts* £2.99
☐ 1–85283–875-X *The Factfile* £2.99

*All these books are available at your local bookshop or newsagent, or can be ordered direct from the publisher. Just tick the titles you want and fill in the form below.*

*Prices and availability subject to change without notice.*

Boxtree Cash Sales, P.O. Box 11, Falmouth, Cornwall TR10 9EN.

Please send cheque or postal order for the value of the book, and add the following for postage and packing.

**U.K. including B.F.P.O.** – £1.00 for one book, plus 50p for the second book, and 30p for each additional book ordered up to a £3.00 maximum.

**Overseas including Eire** – £2.00 for the first book, plus £1.00 for the second book, and 50p for each additional book ordered.

OR please debit this amount from my Access/Visa Card (delete as appropriate).

Card Number

Amount £ ...........................................................................................

Expiry Date ...........................................................................................

Signed ...........................................................................................

Name ...........................................................................................

Address ...........................................................................................